D0865485

BISON BOOKS

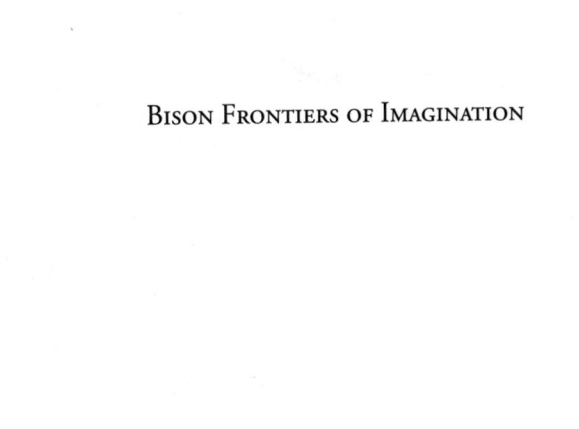

Bison Frontiers of Imagination

Beyond Thirty

Edgar Rice Burroughs

Introduction to the Bison Books Edition by
David Brin

Essays by Phillip R. Burger and Richard A. Lupoff

UNIVERSITY OF NEBRASKA PRESS
LINCOLN AND LONDON

Introduction © 2001 by David Brin

"The War to End All Future Wars" and "Beyond 1965, Beyond 2137, Beyond 30" © 2001 by
the University of Nebraska Press

Manufactured in the United States of America

♾

First Bison Books printing: 2001

Most recent printing indicated by the last digit below:
10   9   8   7   6   5   4   3   2   1

Library of Congress Cataloging-in-Publication Data
Burroughs, Edgar Rice, 1875–1950.
Beyond thirty / Edgar Rice Burroughs; introduction to the Bison Books edition by David
Brin; essays by Phillip R. Burger and Richard A. Lupoff.
p. cm.—(Bison frontiers of imagination)
ISBN 0-8032-6184-5 (pbk.: alk. paper)
1. Imaginary wars and battles—Fiction. 2. Americans—Europe—Fiction. 3.
Europe—Fiction.
I. Title. II. Series.
PS3503.U687 B49 2001
813′.52—dc21   00-051191

Contents

Introduction

"Progress" is a funny thing. Most traditional human civilizations didn't even believe in it. Instead their legends told of some golden time in the deep past when people were wiser and had some of the powers of gods. In fact, the same general fable cropped up so often in so many locales that a number of nineteenth-century mystics reached a quaint conclusion: that all such myths hearken to the same great fallen civilization whose heights will never again be seen by benighted humankind.

Today we know that such legends never referred to a real "Mu" or "Atlantis," no glorious isle that sank into the sea. Instead, all those myths of a past Golden Age seem to have risen naturally as artifacts of human imagination. They were—and continue to be—engendered from within by a combination of romanticism, curmudgeonliness, nostalgia, and the tremulousness that came from living in a dark and capricious world, where Nature's rules are a complete mystery. In such a state, it was only natural to fantasize that someone, sometime, had a better grasp of what was going on.

Ours is one of the few cultures that ever escaped this syndrome, partaking instead of an exceptional and rather irreverent notion—that a golden age of our own creation may lie ahead of us rather than in some lamented past. According to this rebel worldview, each generation of people should be better and more knowing than its predecessors. In other words, we hold that children can learn from their parents' mistakes. They may even move forward a little, making the hard labor of their forebears seem less wasted and more worthwhile.

This new way of looking at things, reversing the age-old *time flow of wisdom*, is an underpinning of both modern science and science fiction. Yes, science fiction does portray many dystopias and dark warnings. Nevertheless, when we *do* dream about golden ages, they are mostly set in some era yet to come. The result is a perfectly delightful tension with time itself, a fascination with both past and future.

It can be humbling to examine the imagined worlds of earlier authors, seeing how often their projections went awry and how, occasionally, they were startlingly ahead of their time. Take for example E. E. Hale's prescient story, "The Brick Moon," published in the *Atlantic Monthly* back in the 1860s, which predicted the use of navigation and communication satellites in geosynchronous orbit! The tale also portrayed those satellites as being manufactured out of *brick* and launched into space by a water-mill-driven flywheel! Expanding this notion dramatically, Hale had the first of these "moons" hurled skyward prematurely, with construction workers and their families aboard. These inadvertent space colonists are sustained in orbit by some atmosphere "dragged along" by the hurtling orb. Then they proceed to "evolve," letting Hale comment favorably (if naively) on the hottest topic of his time, Charles Darwin's recent *On the Origin of Species*. A modern reader can only rock back and forth between hilarity and awe, ultimately marveling at Hale's amazing vision.

Another grand rediscovery from the past is the work you now hold, Edgar Rice Burroughs's *Beyond Thirty*. One of the author's earliest works, it appeared briefly in an obscure magazine and thereafter became an object of fevered interest by Burroughs fans across the world, who would barter precious smudged mimeographs and hand-typed, pirated editions. Between its first appearance and this one, there were only two minor reprintings: a limited edition in 1957 by Bradford Day and a mass-market paperback in 1970, which Ace Books retitled *The Lost Continent*. In it, however, some of the date references that make the book so interesting were removed. Now, at last, the complete original story is available to modern readers, allowing us to appreciate this lost jewel on several levels at once.

For fans of Burroughs the adventure writer, it is yet another brief, exciting action fix—an escapade in the truest sense, filled with bloodthirsty pursuers and life-and-death struggles along with tense evasions through jungles, forests, and ancient ruins. Naturally, there is the requisite beautiful, resourceful princess to focus our hero's attentions and chaste longings. At this level, *Beyond Thirty* may seem just a bit primitive compared to later Burroughs works. It moves along in satisfying ways but never reveals those brief, startling moments of high-octane writing that Burroughs showed himself capable of in following years.

But never mind. *Beyond Thirty* stands out for other fascinating reasons. For one thing it is a novel of and about a precise moment in time. Although *Beyond Thirty* portrays events taking place centuries in the future, it could have appeared only in the very year that it was published—1916.

The novel is set three hundred years after conflict broke out among the nations of Europe, pulverizing that continent's ancient civilization into amnesia and barbarism. The premise of Burroughs's story, that twenty-third-century Europe had fallen and failed to rise again, was influenced by passions that were coursing through American life during an election year when Woodrow Wilson ran on the slogan "he kept us out of war."

Burroughs presents a simple extrapolation, taking events that had been building ever since the European Great War broke out in 1914 and suggesting their ultimate, logical conclusion. Within the form of an if-this-goes-on story, he foresees the horrifying savagery burgeoning in hatred and violence, hurtling toward an unstoppable orgy of mutual destruction. He also presumes that America's revulsion and isolationism might likewise burgeon, culminating in a fanatical embargo and blockade along the thirtieth degree of longitude (hence the book's title). Fearing contamination, no citizen of the United Western Hemisphere would venture beyond that *cordon sanitaire* for ten generations. That is, until this tale unfolds.

If-this-goes-on is a well-loved subgenre of science fiction, lending itself especially well to political and social satire, but any sensible author knows that straightforward extrapolation seldom predicts history. It's a failing that all would-be seers must live with, and few novels illustrate this caution better than *Beyond Thirty*. Just one year after it was published, America's growing revulsion with events in Europe led *not* toward greater isolation but to willing participation in the violent fray, as part of an effort to "make the world safe for democracy."

Despite efforts by generations of tedious cynics to mock that motive, America's entry into World War I *did* reflect some nobility of spirit. Indeed, the twentieth century might have gone much better had Woodrow Wilson's agenda and warning at the Versailles Peace Conference been more closely heeded. But that is beside the point.

What matters to us here is that Edgar Rice Burroughs felt passionately about the war and possible American involvement. His ambivalence in 1916 about Europe's gruesome war is reflected in the attitude of Lt. Jefferson Turck, the hero of *Beyond Thirty*. Lieutenant Turck—commander of a marvelous flying submarine charged with maintaining the embargo at thirty degrees longitude—disdains the smug isolationism and lack of compassion shown by his vast and thriving nation toward those suffering in distant lands to the east. At the same time though, Turck's sad contempt for the madness that consumed great Europe mirrors the common feeling of 1916 America that something deeply contemptible and nauseating was going on "over there."

Some reviewers have dismissed *Beyond Thirty* as a simple reversal story about Americans sailing east to colonize a Europe filled with savages. But this interpretation is just plain silly. The entire second half of the book, portraying interventions by advanced nations of Africa and Asia, belies this theory. No, the proper subgenre is if-this-goes-on, all right. The book is about Europe—poor, suffering Europe—being ultimately saved from the consequences of its own self-created calamity by the arrival of outsiders, each coming to impose its own style of mercy on the descendants of fools.

While we're on the subject of authorial motives, Edgar Rice Burroughs has also been accused of racism and sexism by latter-day critics, who seem incapable of viewing an author's writings in the context of the times in which they were written. In fact, Burroughs's female characters often show great nobility, cleverness, courage, and self-sacrifice, all traits the author clearly admired. During an age of sharp transition, when many still believed that women should be coddled or kept down, his heroines always displayed both "spunk" and considerable pride, defending themselves capably when necessary, and demanding and getting respect from Burroughs's enlightened heroes.

The racism issue is more difficult. Just as Burroughs reflected America's divided feelings over isolationism in 1916, he also exhibited ambiguity over the ethnic prejudices of his day. The African Empire in *Beyond Thirty* is portrayed with a mixture of cautious respect and worried loathing. The novel's protagonist expresses surprise at the accomplishments of a black nation, and that reaction could be viewed as racist in a modern context. But set against the background of common stereotypes and a virulent Ku Klux Klan revival that was taking place even as Burroughs wrote this book, there can be little doubt where he fell on the tolerance spectrum of his day. He challenged his readers to imagine a different reality, one in which all the pat racial assumptions and blithely assumed power relationships might be upended—and not without justification. That was a daring concept in its day.

Certainly his depiction of a rich, dignified, and illuminated future China—written in an era when other popular authors railed against a "yellow peril"—allows us to settle the ambiguity decisively. Burroughs was not only willing to entertain thoughts of greater equality in the future but eager to portray such transformations in a positive light. He was a propagandist and agitator for change, even if the prospect provoked mixed feelings in his own heart.

It may seem that this is all being taken much too seriously. After all, *Beyond Thirty* is no polemical tract or clarion call. From beginning to end, first and foremost, it is an adventure tale. Certainly its first readers—mostly young white males—saw it that way. If they were swayed toward new thoughts about isolationism or sexual liberation or racial equality, the mental steps were modest and incremental.

But of such bricks new worlds are made. We are living witnesses that *something* nudged the western conscience to move ahead, staggering forward like a well-meaning drunkard toward a rather more honorable level of civilization. To claim that every bit of that progress resulted from direct confrontation is to ignore the great role that myth and legend has always played in human life. Authors who evoke sympathy for others—even masked within a gaudy adventure tale—stoke a growing wish to see the world become different than it is.

Judge for yourself. Welcome to the myth called *Beyond Thirty*. It could have been written in no other year than the one that it was, yet this early Burroughs work contributed an undeniably agreeable thread to the complex weaving of science fiction into twentieth-century life. *Beyond Thirty* is an adventure story worth talking and arguing about. It's about time we got to enjoy this spunky little story once again.

BEYOND THIRTY

Chapter I

Since earliest childhood I have been strangely fascinated by the mystery surrounding the history of the last days of twentieth century Europe. My interest is keenest, perhaps, not so much in relation to known facts as to speculation upon the unknowable of the two centuries that have rolled by since human intercourse between the Western and Eastern Hemispheres ceased—the mystery of Europe's state following the termination of the Great War—provided, of course, that the war had been terminated.

From out the meagerness of our censored histories we learned that for fifteen years after the cessation of diplomatic relations between the United States of North America and the belligerent nations of the Old World, news of more or less doubtful authenticity filtered, from time to time, into the Western Hemisphere from the Eastern.

Then came the fruition of that historic propaganda which is best described by its own slogan: "The East for the East—the West for the West," and all further intercourse was stopped by statute.

Even prior to this, transoceanic commerce had practically ceased, owing to the perils and hazards of the mine-strewn waters of both the Atlantic and Pacific Oceans. Just when submarine activities ended we do not know; but the last vessel of this type sighted by a Pan-American merchantman was the huge Q 138, which discharged twenty-nine torpedoes at a Brazilian tank steamer off the Bermudas in the fall of 1922. A heavy sea and the excellent seamanship of the master of the

Brazilian permitted the Pan-American to escape and report this last of a long series of outrages upon our commerce. God alone knows how many hundreds of our ancient ships fell prey to the roving steel sharks of blood-frenzied Europe. Countless were the vessels and men that passed over our eastern and western horizons never to return; but whether they met their fates before the belching tubes of submarines or among the aimlessly drifting mine fields, no man lived to tell.

And then came the great Pan-American Federation which linked the Western Hemisphere from pole to pole under a single flag, which joined the navies of the New World into the mightiest fighting force that ever sailed the seven seas—the greatest argument for peace the world had ever known.

Since that day peace had reigned from the western shores of the Azores to the western shores of the Hawaiian Islands, nor has any man of either hemisphere dared cross 30W. or 175W. From 30 to 175 is ours—from 30 to 175 is peace, prosperity and happiness.

Beyond was the great unknown. Even the geographies of my boyhood showed nothing beyond. We were taught of nothing beyond. Speculation was discouraged. For two hundred years the Eastern Hemisphere had been wiped from the maps and histories of Pan-America. Its mention in fiction, even, was forbidden.

Our ships of peace patrol 30 and 175. What ships from beyond they have warned only the secret archives of government show; but, a naval officer myself, I have gathered from the traditions of the service that it has been fully two hundred years since smoke or sail has been sighted east of 30 or west of 175. The fate of the relinquished provinces which lay beyond the dead lines we could only speculate upon. That the military power which rose so suddenly in China after the fall of the republic, and which wrested Manchuria and Korea from Russia and Japan, and also absorbed the Phillippines is quite within the range of possibility.

It was the commander of a Chinese man-of-war who received a copy of the edict of 1921 from the hand of my illustrious ancestor, Admiral Turck, on 175, two hundred and six years ago, and from the yellowed pages of the admiral's diary I learned that the fate of the Phillippines were even then presaged by these Chinese naval officers.

Yes, for over two hundred years no man crossed 30 to 175 and lived to tell his story—not until chance drew me across and back again, and public opinion, revolting at last against the drastic regulations of our long-dead forbears, demanded that my story be given to the world, and that the narrow interdict which commanded peace, prosperity, and happiness to halt at 30 and 175 be removed forever.

I am glad that it was given to me to be an instrument in the hands of Providence for the uplifting of benighted Europe, and the amelioration of the suffering, degradation, and abysmal ignorance in which I found her.

I shall not live to see the complete regeneration of the savages hordes of the Eastern Hemisphere—that is a work which will require many generations, perhaps ages, so complete has been their reversion to savagery; but I know that the work has been started, and I am proud of the share in it which my generous countrymen have placed in my hands.

The government already possesses a complete official report of my adventures beyond 30. In the narrative I purpose telling my story in a less formal, and I hope, a more entertaining, style; though, being only a naval officer and without claim to the slightest literary ability, I shall most certainly fall far short of the possibilities which are inherent in my subject. That I have passed through the most wondrous adventures that have befallen a civilized man during the past two centuries encourages me in the belief that, however ill the telling, the facts themselves will command your interest to the final page.

Beyond thirty! Romance, adventure, strange peoples, fearsome beasts —all the excitement and scurry of the lives of the twentieth century ancients that have been denied us in these dull days of peace and prosaic prosperity—all, all lay beyond thirty, the invisible barrier between the stupid, commercial present and the carefree, barbarous past.

What boy has not sighed for the good old days of wars, revolutions, and riots: how I used to pore over the chronicles of those old days, those dear old days, when workmen went armed to their labors; when they fell upon one another with gun and bomb and dagger, and the streets ran red with blood! Ah, but those were the times when life was worth the living: when a man who went out by night knew not at which dark corner a "footpad" might leap upon and slay him; when wild beasts roamed the forest and the jungles, and there were savage men, and countries yet unexplored.

Now, in all the Western Hemisphere dwells no man who may not find a school house within walking distance of his home, or at least within flying distance. The wildest beast that roams our waste places lairs in the frozen north or the frozen south within a government reserve, where the curious may view him and feed him bread crusts from the hand with perfect impunity.

But beyond thirty! And I have gone there, and come back; and now you may go there, for no longer is it high treason, punishable by disgrace or death, to cross 30 or 175.

My name is Jefferson Turck. I am a lieutenant in the navy—in the great Pan-American navy, the only navy which now exists in all the world.

I was born in Arizona, in the United States of North America, in the year of our Lord 2116. Therefore, I am twenty-one years old.

In early boyhood I tired of the teeming cities and over-crowded rural districts of Arizona. Every generation of Turcks for over two centuries has been represented in the navy. The navy called to me, as did the free, wide, un-peopled spaces of the mighty oceans. And so I joined the navy, coming up from the ranks, as we all must, learning our craft as we advance. My promotion was rapid, for my family seems to inherit naval lore. We are born officers, and I reserve to myself no special credit for an early advancement in the service.

At twenty I found myself a lieutenant in command of the aero-submarine *Coldwater*, of the SS-96 class. The *Coldwater* was one of the first of the air and under-water craft which have been so greatly improved since its launching, and was possessed of innumerable weaknesses which, fortunately, have been eliminated in more recent vessels of similar type.

Even when I took command, she was fit only for the junk pile; but the world-old parsimony of government retained her in active service, and sent two hundred men to sea in her, with myself, a mere boy, in command of her, to patrol 30 from Iceland to the Azores.

Much of my service had been spent aboard the great merchantmen-of-war. These are the utility naval vessels that have transformed the navies of old, which burdened the peoples with taxes for their support, into the present day fleets of self-supporting ships that find ample time for target practice and gun drill while they bear freight and the mails from the continents to the far-scattered island of Pan-America.

This change in service was most welcome to me, especially as it brought with it coveted responsibilities of sole command, and I was prone to overlook the deficiencies of the *Coldwater* in the natural pride I felt in my first ship.

The *Coldwater* was fully equipped for two months patrolling—the ordinary length of assignment to this service—and a month had already passed, its monotony entirely unrelieved by sight of another craft, when the first of our misfortunes befell.

We had been riding out a storm at an altitude of about three thousand feet. All night we had hovered above the tossing billows of the moonlit clouds. The detonation of the thunder and the glare of lightning through an occasional rift in the vaporous wall proclaimed the continued fury of the tempest upon the surface of the sea; but we, far above it all, rode in comparative ease upon the upper gale. With the coming of dawn the clouds beneath us became a glorious sea of gold and silver, soft and beautiful; but they could not deceive us as to the blackness and the terrors of the storm-lashed ocean which they hid.

I was at breakfast when my chief engineer entered and saluted. His face was grave, and I thought he was even a trifle paler than usual.

"Well?" I asked.

He drew the back of his forefinger nervously across his brown in a gesture that was habitual with him in moments of mental stress.

"The gravitation-screen generators, sir," he said. "Number one went to the bad about an hour and a half ago. We have been working upon it steadily since; but I have to report, sir, that it is beyond repair."

"Number two will keep us supplied," I answered. "In the meantime we will send a wireless for relief."

"But that is the trouble, sir," he went on. "Number two has stopped. I knew it would come, sir. I made a report on these generators three years ago. I advised then that they both be scrapped. Their principle is entirely wrong. They're done for;" and, with a grim smile, "I shall at least have the satisfaction of knowing my report was accurate."

"Have we sufficient reserve screen to permit us to make land, or, at least, meet our relief halfway?" I asked.

"No, sir," he replied gravely; "we are sinking now."

"Have you anything further to report?" I asked.

"No, sir," he said.

"Very good," I replied; and, as I dismissed him, I rang for my wireless operator. When he appeared, I gave him a message to the secretary of the navy, to whom all vessels in service on 30 and 175 report direct. I explained our predicament, and stated that with what screening force remained I should continue in the air, making as rapid headway toward St. Johns as possible, and that when we were forced to take to the water I should continue in the same direction.

The accident occurred directly over 30 and about 52 N. The surface wind was blowing a tempest from the west. To attempt to ride out such a storm upon the surface seemed suicidal, for the *Coldwater* was not designed for surface navigation except under fair weather conditions. Submerged, or in the air, she was tractable enough in any sort of weather when under control; but without her screen generators she was almost helpless, since she could not fly, and, if submerged, could not rise to the surface.

All these defects have been remedied in later models; but the knowledge did not help us any that day aboard the slowly settling *Coldwater*, with an angry sea roaring beneath, a tempest ranging out of the west, and 30 only a few knots astern.

To cross 30 or 175 has been, as you know, the direst calamity that could befall a naval commander. Court-martial and degradation follow swiftly, unless as is often the case, the unfortunate man takes his own life before this unjust and heartless regulation can hold him up to public scorn.

There has been in the past no excuse, no circumstance, that could palliate the offense.

"He was in command, and he took his ship across 30!" That was sufficient. It might not have been in any way his fault, as, in the case of the *Coldwater*, it could not possibly have been justly charged to my account that the gravitation-screen generators were worthless; but well I knew that should chance have it that we were blown across 30 today—

as we might easily be before the terrific west wind that we could hear howling below us, the responsibility would fall upon my shoulders.

In a way, the regulation was a good one, for it certainly accomplished that for which it was intended. We all fought shy of 30 on the east and 175 on the west, and, though we had to skirt them pretty close, nothing but an act of God ever drew one of us across. You all are familiar with the naval tradition that a good officer could sense proximity to either line, and for my part, I am firmly convinced of the truth of this as I am that the compass finds the north without recourse to tedious processes of reasoning.

Old Admiral Sanchez was wont to maintain that he could smell 30, and the men of the first ship in which I sailed claimed that Coburn, the navigating officer, knew by name every wave along 30 from 60 N. to 60 S. However, I'd hate to vouch for this.

Well, to get back to my narrative; we kept on dropping slowly toward the surface the while we bucked the west wind, clawing away from 30 as fast as we could. I was on the bridge, and as we dropped from the brilliant sunlight into the dense vapor of clouds and on down through them to the wild, dark storm strata beneath, it seemed that my spirits dropped with the falling ship, and the buoyancy of hope ran low in sympathy.

The waves were running to tremendous heights, and the *Coldwater* was not designed to meet such waves head on. Her elements were the blue ether, far above the raging storm, or the greater depths of ocean, which no storm could ruffle.

As I stood speculating upon our chances once we settled into the frightful Maelstrom beneath us and at the same time mentally computing the hours which must elapse before aid could reach us, the wireless operator clambered up the ladder to the bridge, and, disheveled and breathless, stood before me at salute. It needed by a glance at him to assure me that something was amiss.

"What now?" I asked.

"The wireless, sir!" he cried. "My God, sir, I cannot send."

"But the emergency outfit?" I asked.

"I have tried everything, sir. I have exhausted every resource. We cannot send," and he drew himself up and saluted again.

I dismissed him with a few kind words, for I knew that it was through no fault of his that the mechanism was antiquated and worthless, in common with the balance of the *Coldwater's* equipment. There was no finer operator in Pan-America than he.

The failure of the wireless did not appear as momentous to me as to him, which is not unnatural, since it is but human to feel that when our own little cog slips the entire universe must necessarily be put out of gear. I knew that if this storm was destined to blow us across 30, or send us to the bottom of the ocean, no help could reach us in time to prevent. I had ordered the message sent solely because regulations required it, and not with any particular hope that we could benefit by it in our present extremity.

I had little time to dwell upon the coincidence of the simultaneous failure of the wireless and the buoyancy generators, since very shortly after the *Coldwater* had dropped so low over the waters that all my attention was necessarily centered upon the delicate business of settling upon the waves without breaking my ship's back. With our buoyancy generators in commission it would have been a simple thing to enter the water, since then it would have been but a trifling matter of a forty-five degree dive into the base of a huge wave. We should have cut into the water like a hot knife through butter, and been totally submerged with scarce a jar—I have done it a thousand times—but I did not dare submerge the *Coldwater* for fear that it would remain submerged to the end of time—a condition far from conductive to the longevity of commander or crew.

Most of my officers were older men than I. John Alvarez, my first officer, is twenty years my senior. He stood at my side on the bridge as the ship glided closer and closer to those stupendous waves. He watched my every move, but he was by far too fine an officer and gentleman to embarrass me by either comment or suggestion.

When I saw that we soon would touch, I ordered the ship brought around broadside to the wind, and there we hovered a moment until a huge wave reached up and seized us upon its crest, and then I gave the order that suddenly reversed the screening force, and let us into the ocean. Down into the trough we went, wallowing like the carcass of a dead whale, and then began the fight, with rudder and propellers, to force the *Coldwater* back into the teeth of the gale and drive her on and on, farther and farther from relentless 30.

I think that we should have succeeded, even though the ship was wracked from stem to stern by the terrific buffetings she received, and though she were half submerged the greater part of the time, had no further accident befallen us.

We were making headway, though slowly, and it began to look as though we were going to pull through. Alvarez never left my side, though I all but ordered him below for much-needed rest. My second officer, Porfirio Johnson, was also often on the bridge. He was a good officer, but a man for whom I had conceived a rather unreasoning aversion which was not lessened by the knowledge which I subsequently gained that he looked upon my rapid promotion with jealousy. He was ten years my senior both in years and service, and I rather think he could never forget the fact that he had been an officer when I was a green apprentice.

As it became more and more apparent that the *Coldwater*, under my seamanship, was weathering the tempest and giving promise of pulling through safely, I could have sworn that I perceived a shade of annoyance and disappointment growing upon his dark countenance. He left the bridge finally and went below. I do not know that he is directly responsible for what followed so shortly after; but I have always had my suspicions, and Alvarez is even more prone to place the blame upon him than I.

It was about six bells of the forenoon watch that Johnson returned to the bridge after an absence of some thirty minutes. He seemed nervous and ill at ease—a fact which made little impression on me at the time, but which both Alvarez and I recalled subsequently.

Not three minutes after his reappearance at my side the *Coldwater* suddenly commenced to lose headway. I seized the telephone at my elbow, pressing upon the button which would call the chief engineer to the instrument in the bowels of the ship, only to find him already at the receiver attempting to reach me.

"Numbers one, two, and five engines have broken down, sir," he called. "Shall we force the remaining three?"

"We can do nothing else," I bellowed into the transmitter.

"They won't stand the gaff, sir," he returned.

"Can you suggest a better plan?" I asked.

"No, sir," he replied.

"Then give them the gaff, lieutenant," I shouted back, and hung up the receiver.

For twenty minutes the *Coldwater* bucked the great seas with her three engines. I doubt if she advanced a foot; but it was enough to keep her nose in the wind, and, at least, we were not drifting toward 30.

Johnson and Alvarez were at my side when, without warning, the bow swung swiftly around and the ship fell into the trough of the sea.

"The other three have gone," I said, and I happened to be looking at Johnson as I spoke. Was it the shadow of a satisfied smile that crossed his thin lips? I do not know; but at least he did not weep.

"You always have been curious, sir, about the great unknown beyond 30," he said. "You are in a good way to have your curiosity satisfied." And then I could not mistake the slight sneer that curved his upper lip. There must have been a trace of disrespect in his tone or manner which escaped me, for Alvarez turned upon him like a flash.

"When Lieutenant Turck crosses 30," he said, "we shall all cross with him, and God help the officer or the man who reproaches him!"

"I shall not be a party to high treason," snapped Johnson. "The regulations are explicit, and if the *Coldwater* crosses 30 it devolves upon you to place Lieutenant Turck under arrest and immediately exert every endeavor to bring the ship back into Pan-American waters."

"I shall not know," replied Alvarez, "that the *Coldwater* passes 30; nor shall any other man aboard know it," and, with his words, he drew a revolver from his pocket, and before either I or Johnson could prevent it had put a bullet into every instrument upon the bridge, ruining them beyond repair.

And then he saluted me, and strode from the bridge, a martyr to loyalty and friendship, for, though no man might know that Lieutenant Jefferson Turck had taken his ship across 30, every man aboard would know that the first officer had committed a crime that was punishable by both degradation and death. Johnson turned and eyed me narrowly.

"Shall I place him under arrest?" he asked.

"You shall not," I replied. "Nor shall anyone else."

"You become a party to his crime!" he cried angrily.

"You may go below, Mr. Johnson," I said, "and attend to the work of unpacking the extra instruments and having them properly set upon the bridge."

He saluted, and left me, and for some time I stood, gazing out upon the angry waters, my mind filled with unhappy reflections upon the unjust fate that had overtaken me, and the sorrow and disgrace that I had unwittingly brought down upon my house.

I rejoiced that I should leave neither wife nor child to bear the burden of my shame throughout their lives.

As I thought upon my misfortune, I considered more clearly than ever before the unrighteousness of the regulation which was to prove my doom, and in the natural revolt against its injustice my anger rose, and there mounted within me a feeling which I imagine must have paralleled that spirit that once was prevalent among the ancients called anarchy.

For the first time in my life I found my sentiments arraying themselves against custom, tradition, and even government. The wave of rebellion swept over me in an instant, beginning with an heretical doubt as to the sanctity of the established order of things—that fetish which has ruled Pan-Americans for two centuries, and which is based upon a blind faith in the infallibility of the prescience of the long-dead framers of the articles of Pan-American federation—and ending in an adamantine determination to defend my honor and my life to the last ditch against the blind and senseless regulation which assumed the synonymity of misfortune and treason.

I would replace the destroyed instruments upon the bridge; every officer and man should know when we crossed 30. But then I should assert the spirit which dominated me, I should resist arrest, and insist upon bringing my ship back across the dead line, remaining at my post until we had reached New York. Then I should make a full report, and with it a demand upon public opinion that the dead lines be wiped forever from the seas.

I knew that I was right—I knew that no more loyal officer wore the uniform of the navy—I knew that I was a good officer and sailor, and I didn't propose submitting to degradation and discharge because a lot of old, preglacial fossils had declared over two hundred years before that no man should cross 30.

Even while these thoughts were passing through my mind I was busy with the details of my duties. I had seen to it that a sea anchor was rigged, and even now the men had completed their task, and the *Coldwater* was swinging around rapidly, her nose pointing once more into the wind, and the frightful rolling consequent upon her wallowing in the trough was happily diminished.

It was then that Johnson came hurrying to the bridge. One of his eyes was swollen and already darkening, and his lip was cut and bleeding. Without even the formality of a salute, he burst upon me, white with fury.

"Lieutenant Alvarez attacked me!" he cried. "I demand that he be placed under arrest. I found him in the act of destroying the reserve instruments, and when I would have interfered to protect them he fell upon me and beat me. I demand that you arrest him!"

"You forget yourself, Mr. Johnson," I said. "You are not in command of the ship. I deplore the action of Lieutenant Alvarez, but I cannot expunge from my mind the loyalty and self-sacrificing friendship which has prompted him to his acts. Were I you, sir, I should profit by the example he has set. Further, Mr. Johnson, I intend retaining command of the ship, even though she crosses 30, and I shall demand implicit obedience from every officer and man aboard until I am properly relieved from duty by a superior officer in the port of New York."

"You mean to say that you will cross 30 without submitting to arrest?" he almost shouted.

"I do, sir," I replied: "and now you may go below, and when again you find it necessary to address me, you will please be so good as to bear in mind the fact that I am your commanding officer, and as such entitled to a salute."

He flushed, hesitated a moment, and then, saluting, turned upon his heel and left the bridge. Shortly after, Alvarez appeared. He was pale, and seemed to have aged ten years in the few brief minutes since I last had seen him. Saluting, he told me very simply what he had done, and asked that I place him under arrest.

I put my hand on his shoulder, and I guess that my voice trembled a trifle as, while reproving him for his act, I made it plain to him that my gratitude was no less potent a force than his loyalty to me. Then it was that I outlined to him my purpose to defy the regulation that had raised the dead lines, and to take my ship back to New York myself.

I did not ask him to share the responsibility with me. I merely stated that I should refuse to submit to arrest, and that I should demand of him and every other officer and man implicit obedience to my every command until we docked at home.

His face brightened at my words, and he assured me that I would find him as ready to acknowledge my command upon the wrong side of 30 as upon the right, an assurance which I hastened to tell him I did not need.

The storm continued to rage for three days, and as far as the wind scarce varied a point during all that time, I knew that we must be far beyond 30, drifting rapidly east by south. All this time it had been impossible to work upon the damaged engines or the gravity-screen generators; but we had a full set of instruments upon the bridge, for Alvarez, after discovering my intentions, had fetched the reserve instruments from his own cabin, where he had hidden them. Those which Johnson had seen him destroy had been a third set which only Alvarez had known were aboard the *Coldwater*.

We waited impatiently for the sun, that we might determine our exact location, and upon the fourth day our vigil was rewarded a few minutes before noon.

Every officer and man aboard was tense with nervous excitement as we awaited the result of the reading. The crew had known almost as soon as I that we were doomed to cross 30, and I am inclined to believe that every man jack of them was tickled to death, for the spirits of adventure and romance still live in the hearts of men of the twenty-second century, even though there be little for them to feed upon between 30 and 175.

The men carried none of the burdens of responsibility—they might cross 30 with impunity, and doubtless they would return to be heroes at home; but how different the homecoming of their commanding officer!

The wind had dropped to a steady blow, still from west by north, and the sea had gone down correspondingly. The crew, with the exception of those whose duties kept them below, were ranged on deck below the bridge. When our position was definitely fixed I personally announced it to the eager, waiting men.

"Men," I said, stepping forward to the handrail and looking down into their upturned, bronzed faces, "you are anxiously awaiting information as to the ship's position. It has been determined at latitude fifty degrees seven minutes north, longitude twenty degrees sixteen minutes west."

I paused and a buzz of animated comment ran through the massed men beneath me. "Beyond 30: but there will be no change in commanding officers, in routine or in discipline, until after we have docked again in New York."

As I ceased speaking and stepped back from the rail there was a roar of applause from the deck such as I never before had heard abroad a ship of peace. It recalled to my mind tales that I had read of the good old days when naval vessels were built to fight, when ships of peace had been man-of-war, and guns had flashed in other than futile target practice, and decks had run red with blood.

With the subsidence of the sea, we were able to go to work upon the damaged engines to some effect, and I also set men to examining the gravitation-screen generators with a view to putting them in working order should it prove not beyond our resources.

For two weeks we labored at the engines, which indisputably showed evidence of having been tampered with. I appointed a board to investigate and report upon the disaster; but it accomplished nothing other than to convince me that there were several officers upon it who were in full sympathy with Johnson, for, though no charges had been preferred against him, the board went out of its way specifically to exonerate him in its findings.

All this time we were drifting almost due east. The work upon the engines had progressed to such an extent that within a few hours we might expect to be able to proceed under our own power to the westward in the direction of Pan-American waters.

To relieve the monotony I had taken to fishing, and early that morning I had departed from the *Coldwater* in one of the boats on such an excursion. A gentle west wind was blowing. The sea shimmered in the sunlight. A cloudless sky canopied us. With only a small compass to guide us, we bore toward the west for our sport, as I had made it a point never voluntarily to make an inch toward the east that I could avoid—at least, they should not be able to charge me with a wilful violation of the dead lines regulation.

I had with me only the boat's ordinary complement of men—three in all, and more than enough to handle any small power boat. I had not asked any of my officers to accompany me, as I wished to be alone, and very glad am I now that I had not. My only regret is that, in view of what befell us, it had been necessary to bring the three brave fellows who manned the boat.

Our fishing, which proved excellent, carried us so far to the west that we no longer could see the *Coldwater*. The day wore on, until at last, about mid-afternoon, I gave the order to return to the ship.

We had proceeded but a short distance toward the east when one of the men gave an exclamation of excitement, at the same time pointing eastward. We all looked in the direction he had indicated, and there, a short distance above the horizon, we saw the outlines of the *Coldwater* silhouetted against the sky.

"They've repaired the engines and the generators both," exclaimed one of the men.

It seemed impossible, but yet it had evidently been done. Only that morning, Lieutenant Johnson had told me that he feared that it would be impossible to repair the generators. I had put him in charge of this work, since he always had been accounted one of the best gravitation-screen men in the navy. He had invented several of the improvements that are incorporated in the later models of these generators, and I am convinced that he knows more concerning both the theory and the practice of screening gravitation than any living Pan-American.

At the sight of the *Coldwater* once more under control, the three men burst into a glad cheer; but, for some reason for which I could not then account, I was strangely overcome by a premonition of personal misfortune. It was not that I now anticipated an early return to Pan-America and a board of inquiry, for I had rather looked forward to the fight that must follow my return. No, there was something else, something indefinable and vague that cast a strange gloom upon me as I saw my ship rising farther above the water and making straight in our direction.

I was not long in ascertaining a possible explanation of my depression, for, though we were plainly visible from the bridge of the aero-submarine and to the hundreds of men who swarmed her deck, the ship passed directly above us, not five hundred feet from the water, and sped directly westward.

We all shouted, and I fired my pistol to attract their attention, though I knew full well that all who cared to had observed us, but the ship moved steadily away, growing smaller and smaller to our view until at last she passed complete-out of sight.

Chapter II

What could it mean? I had left Alvarez in command. He was my most loyal subordinate. It was absolutely beyond the pale of possibility that Alvarez should desert me. No, there was some other explanation. Something occurred to place my second officer, Porfirio Johnson, in command—I was sure of it; but why speculate? The futility of conjecture was only too palpable. The *Coldwater* has abandoned us in mid ocean. Doubtless none of us would survive to know why.

The young man at the wheel of the power boat had turned her nose about as it became evident that the ship intended passing over us, and now he still held her in futile pursuit of the *Coldwater*.

"Bring her about, Snider," I directed, "and hold her due east. We can't catch the *Coldwater*, and we can't cross the Atlantic in this. Our only hope lies in making the nearest land, which, unless I am mistaken, is the Scilly Islands, off the southwest coast of England. Ever heard of England, Snider?"

"There's a part of the United States of North America that used to be known to the ancients as New England," he replied. "Is that where you mean, sir?"

"No, Snider,' I replied. "The England I refer to was an island off the continent of Europe. It was the seat of a very powerful kingdom that flourished over two hundred years ago. A part of the United States of North America and all of the Federated States of Canada once belonged to this ancient England."

"Europe," breathed one of the men, his voice tense with excitement.

"My grandfather used to tell me stories of the world beyond 30. He had been a great student, and he had read much from forbidden books."

"In which I resemble your grandfather," I said, "for I, too, have read more even than naval officers are supposed to read, and, as you men know, we are permitted a greater latitude in the study of geography and history than men of other professions.

"Among the books and papers of Admiral Porter Turck, who lived two hundred years ago, and from whom I am descended, many volumes still exist, and are in my possession, which deal with the history and geography of ancient Europe. Usually I bring several of these books with me upon a cruise, and this time, among others, I have maps of Europe and her surrounding waters. I was studying them as we came away from the *Coldwater* this morning, and luckily I have them with me."

"You are going to try to make Europe, sir?" asked Taylor, the young man who had last spoken.

"It is the nearest land," I replied. "I have always wanted to explore the forgotten lands of the Eastern Hemisphere. Here's our chance. To remain at sea is to perish. None of us ever will see home again. Let us make the best of it, and enjoy while we do live that which is forbidden the balance of our race—the adventure and the mystery which lie beyond 30."

Taylor and Delcarte seized the spirit of my mood; but Snider, I think, was a trifle sceptical.

"It is treason, sir," I replied; "but there is no law which compels us to visit punishment upon ourselves. Could we return to Pan-America, I should be the first to insist that we face it; but we know that's not possible. Even if this craft would carry us so far, we haven't enough water or food for more than three days.

"We are doomed, Snider, to die far from home and without ever again looking upon the face of another fellow countryman than those who sit here now in this boat. Isn't that punishment sufficient for even the most exacting judge?"

Even Snider had to admit that it was.

"Very well, then, let us live while we live, and enjoy to the fullest whatever of adventure or pleasure each new day brings, since any day may be our last, and we shall be dead for a considerable while."

I could see that Snider was still fearful; but Taylor and Delcarte responded with a hearty, "Aye, aye, sir!"

They were of different mold. Both were sons of naval officers. They represented the aristocracy of birth, and they dared to think for themselves.

Snider was in the minority, and so we continued toward the east. Beyond 30, and separated from my ship, my authority ceased. I held leadership, if I was to hold it at all, by virtue of personal qualifications only; but I did not doubt my ability to remain the director of our destinies in so far as they were amenable to human agencies. I have always led. While my brain and brawn remain unimpaired I shall continue always to lead. Following is an art which Turcks do not easily learn.

It was not until the third day that we raised land, dead ahead, which I took, from my map, to be the isles of Scilly; but such a gale was blowing that I did not dare attempt to land, and so we passed to the north of them, skirted Land's End, and entered the English Channel.

I think that up to that moment I had never experienced such a thrill as passed through me when I realized that I was navigating those historic waters. The lifelong dreams that I never had dared hope to see fulfilled were at last a reality; but under what forlorn circumstances!

Never could I return to my native land. To the end of my days I must remain in exile. Yet even these thoughts failed to dampen my ardor.

My eyes scanned the waters. To the north I could see the rockbound coast of Cornwall. Mine were the first American eyes to rest upon it for more than two hundred years. In vain I searched for some sign of ancient commerce that, if history is to be believed, must have dotted the bosom of the Channel with white sails and blackened the heavens with the smoke of countless funnels; but as far as eye could reach the tossing waters of the Channel were empty and deserted.

Toward midnight the wind and sea abated, so that shortly after dawn I determined to make inshore in an attempt to effect a landing, for we were sadly in need of fresh water and food.

According to my observations, we were just off Ram Head, and it was my intention to enter Plymouth Bay and visit Plymouth. From my map it appeared that this city lay back from the coast a short distance;

and there was another city given as Devonport, which appeared to lie at the mouth of the river Tamar.

However, I knew that it would make little difference which city we entered, as the English People were famed of old for their hospitality toward visiting mariners. As we approached the mouth of the bay I looked for the fishing craft which I expected to see emerging thus early in the day for their labors; but even after we rounded Ram Head and were well within the waters of the bay I saw no vessel, neither was there buoy nor light nor any other mark to show larger ships the channel, and I wondered much at this.

The coast was densely overgrown, nor was any building or sign of man apparent from the water. Up the bay and into the River Tamar we motored through a solitude as unbroken as that which rested upon the waters of the channel. For all we could see, there was no indication that man had ever set his foot upon this silent coast.

I was nonplused, and then, for the first time, there crept over me an intuition of the truth.

Here was no sign of war. As far as this portion of the Devon coast was concerned, that seemed to have been over for many years; but neither were there any people, yet I could not find it within myself to believe that I should find no inhabitants in England. Reasoning thus, I discovered that it was improbable that a state of war still existed, and that the people all had been drawn from this portion of England to some other, where they might better defend themselves against an invader.

But what of their ancient coast defenses? What was there here in Plymouth Bay to prevent an enemy landing in force and marching where they wished? Nothing. I could not believe that any enlightened military nation, such as the ancient English are reputed to have been, would have voluntarily so deserted an exposed coast and an excellent harbor to the mercies of an enemy.

I found myself becoming more and more deeply involved in quandary. The puzzle which confronted me I could not unravel. We had landed, and I now stood upon the spot where, according to my map, a large city should rear its spires and chimneys. There was nothing but rough, broken ground covered densely with weeds and brambles, and tall, rank, grass.

Had a city ever stood there, no sign of it remained. The roughness and unevenness of the ground suggested something of a great mass of debris hidden by the accumulation of centuries of undergrowth.

I drew the short cutlass with which both officers and men of the navy are, as you know, armed out of courtesy to the traditions and memories of the past, and with its point dug into the loam about the roots of the vegetation growing at my feet.

The blade entered the soil for a matter of seven inches, when it struck upon something stonelike. Digging about the obstacle, I presently loosened it, and when I had withdrawn it from its sepulcher I found the thing to be an ancient brick of clay, baked in an oven.

Delcarte we had left in charge of the boat; but Snider and Taylor were with me, and, following my example, each engaged in the fascinating sport of prospecting for antiques. Each of us uncovered a great number of these bricks, until we commenced to weary of the monotony of it, when Snider suddenly gave an exclamation of excitement, and, as I turned to look, he held up a human skull for my inspection.

I took it from him and examined it. Directly in the center of the forehead was a small round hole. The gentleman had evidently come to his end defending his country from an invader.

Snider again held aloft another trophy of the search—a metal spike and some tarnished and corroded metal ornaments. They had lain close beside the skull.

With the point of his cutlass Snider scraped the dirt and verdigris from the face of the larger ornament.

"An inscription," he said, and handed the thing to me.

They were the spike and ornaments of an ancient German helmet. Before long we had uncovered many other indications that a great battle had been fought upon the ground where we stood; but I was then and still am at loss to account for the presence of German soldiers upon the English coast so far from London, which history suggests would have been the natural goal of an invader.

I can only account for it by assuming that either England was temporarily conquered by the Teutons, or that an invasion of so fast proportions was undertaken that German troops were hurled upon the English coast in huge numbers and that landings were necessarily effected at many places simultaneously. Subsequent discoveries tend to strengthen this view.

We dug about for a short time with our cutlasses until I became convinced that a city had stood upon the spot at some time in the past, and that beneath our feet, crumbled and dead, lay ancient Devonport.

I could not repress a sigh at the thought of the havoc war had wrought in this part of England, at least. Farther east, nearer London, we should find things very different. There would be the civilization that two centuries must have wrought upon our English cousins as they had upon us. There would be mighty cities, cultivated fields, happy people. There we would be welcomed as long-lost brothers. There would we find a great nation anxious to learn of the world beyond their side of 30, as I had been anxious to learn of that which lay beyond our side of the dead line.

I turned back toward the boat.

"Come, men!" I said. "We will go up the river and fill our casks with fresh water, search for food and fuel, and then tomorrow be in readiness to push on toward the east. I am going to London."

Chapter III

The report of a gun blasted the silence of a dead Devonport with startling abruptness.

It came from the direction of the launch, and in an instant we three were running for the boat as fast as our legs would carry us. As we came in sight of it we saw Delcarte a hundred yards inland from the launch, leaning over something which lay upon the ground. As we called to him he waved his cap, and, stooping, lifted a small deer for our inspection.

I was about to congratulate him on his trophy when we were startled by a horrid, half-human, half-bestial scream a little ahead and to the right of us. It seemed to come from a clump of rank and tangled brush not far from where Delcarte stood. It was a horrid, fearsome sound, the like of which never had fallen upon my ears before.

We looked in the direction from which it came. The smile had died from Delcarte's lips. Even at the distance we were from him I saw his face go suddenly white, and he quickly threw his rifle to his shoulder. At the same moment the thing that had given tongue to the cry moved from the concealing brushwood far enough for us, too, to see it.

Both Taylor and Snider gave little gasps of astonishment and dismay.

"What is it, sir?" asked the latter.

The creature stood about the height of a tall man's waist at the shoulders, and was long and gaunt and sinuous, and with a tawny coat striped with black, and with white throat and belly. In conformation it was similar to a cat—a huge cat, exaggerated colossal cat, with fiendish eyes and the most devilish cast of countenance, as it wrinkled its bristling snout and bared its great yellow fangs.

It was pacing, or rather, slinking, straight for Delcarte, who had now leveled his rifle upon it.

"What is it, sir?" mumbled Snider again, and then a half-forgotten picture from an old natural history sprang to my mind, and I recognized in the frightful beast the Felis tigris of ancient Asia, specimens of which had, in former centuries, been exhibited in the Western Hemisphere.

Snider and Taylor were armed with rifles and revolvers, while I carried only a revolver. Seizing Snider's rifle from his trembling hands, I called to Taylor to follow me, and together we ran forward, shouting, to attract the beast's attention from Delcarte until we should all be quite close enough to attack with the greatest assurance of success.

I cried to Delcarte not to fire until we reached his side, for I was fearful lest our small caliber, steel-jacketed bullets should, far from killing the beast, tend merely to enrage it still further. But he misunderstood me, thinking that I had ordered him to fire.

With the report of his rifle the tiger stopped short in apparent surprise, then turned and bit savagely at its shoulder for an instant, after which it wheeled again toward Delcarte, issuing the most terrific roars and screams, and launched itself, with incredible speed, toward the brave fellow, who now stood his ground pumping bullets from his automatic rifle as rapidly as the weapon would fire.

Taylor and I also opened up on the creature, and as it was broadside to us it offered a splendid target, though for all the impression we appeared to make upon the great cat we might as well have been launching soap bubbles at it.

Straight as a torpedo it rushed for Delcarte, and, as Taylor and I stumbled on through the tall grass toward our unfortunate comrade, we saw the tiger rear upon him and crush him to the earth.

Not a backward step had the noble Delcarte taken. Two hundred years of peace had not sapped the red blood from his courageous line. He went down beneath that avalanche of bestial savagery still working his gun and with his face toward his antagonist. Even in the instant that I thought him dead I could not help but feel a thrill of pride that he was one of my men—one of my class, a Pan-American gentleman of birth, and that he had demonstrated one of the principle contentions of the army-and-navy adherents—that military training was necessary for the salvation of personal courage in the Pan-American race which for generations had had to face no dangers more grave than those incident to ordinary life in a highly civilized community, safeguarded by every means at the disposal of a perfectly organized and all-powerful government utilizing the best that advanced science could suggest.

As we ran toward Delcarte, both Taylor and I were struck by the fact that the beast upon him appeared not to be mauling him, but lay quiet and motionless upon its prey, and when we were quite close, and the muzzles of our guns were at the animal's head, I saw the explanation of this sudden cessation of hostilities—Felis tigris was dead.

One of our bullets, or one of the last that Delcarte fired, had penetrated the heart, and the beast had died even as it sprawled forward crushing Delcarte to the ground.

A moment later, with our assistance, the man had scrambled from beneath the carcass of his would-be slayer, without a scratch to indicate how close to death he had been.

Delcarte's buoyancy was entirely unruffled. He came from under the tiger with a broad grin on his handsome face, nor could I perceive that a muscle trembled or that his voice showed the least indication of nervousness or excitement.

With the termination of the adventure, we began to speculate upon the explanation of the presence of this savage brute at large so great a distance from its native habitat. My readings had taught me that it was practically unknown outside of Asia, and that, so late as the twentieth century, at least, there had been no savage beasts outside captivity in England.

As we talked, Snider joined us, and I returned his rifle to him. Taylor and Delcarte picked up the slain deer, and we all started down toward the launch, walking slowly. Delcarte wanted to fetch the tiger's skin; but I had to deny him permission, since we had no means to properly cure it.

Upon the beach, we skinned the deer and cut away as much meat as we thought we could dispose of, and as we were again embarking to continue up the river for fresh water and fuel, we were startled by a series of screams from the bushes a short distance away.

"Another Felis tigris," said Taylor.

"Or a dozen of them," supplemented Delcarte, and, even as he spoke, there leaped into sight, one after another, eight of the beasts — full grown, magnificent specimens.

At sight of us, they came charging down like infuriated demons. I saw that three rifles would be no match for them, and so I gave the word to put out from shore, hoping that the "tiger," as the ancients called him, could not swim.

Sure enough, they all halted at the beach, pacing back and forth, uttering fiendish cries, and glaring at us in the most malevolent manner.

As we motored away, we presently heard the calls of similar animals far inland. They seemed to be answering the cries of their fellows at the water's edge, and from the wide distribution an great volume of the sound we came to the conclusion that enormous numbers of these beasts must roam the adjacent country.

"They have eaten up the inhabitants," murmured Snider, shuddering.

"I imagine you are right," I agreed, "for their extreme boldness and fearlessness in the presence of man would suggest either that man is entirely unknown to them, or that they are extremely familiar with him as their natural and most easily procured prey."

"But where did they come from?" asked Delcarte. "Could they have traveled here from Asia?"

I shook my head. The thing was a puzzle to me. I knew that it was practically beyond reason to imagine that tigers had crossed the mountain ranges and rivers and all the great continent of Europe to travel this far from their native lairs, and entirely impossible that they should have crossed the English Channel at all. Yet here they were, and in great numbers.

We continued up the Tamar several miles, filled our casks, and then landed to cook some of our deer steak, and have the first square meal that had fallen to our lot since the *Coldwater* deserted us. But scarce had we built our fire and prepared the meat for cooking than Snider, whose eyes had been constantly roving about the landscape from the moment that we left the launch, touched me on the arm and pointed to a clump of bushes which grew a couple of hundred yards away.

Half concealed behind their screening foliage I saw the yellow and black of a big tiger, and, as I looked, the beast stalked majestically toward us. A moment later, he was followed by another and another, and it is needless to state that we beat a hasty retreat to the launch.

The country was apparently infested by these huge carnivora, for after three other attempts to land and cook our food we were forced to abandon the idea entirely, as each time we were driven off by hunting tigers.

It was also equally impossible to obtain the necessary ingredients for our chemical fuel, and, as we had very little left aboard, we determined to step our folding mast and proceed under sail, hoarding our fuel supply for use in emergencies.

I may say that it was with no regret that we bid adieu to Tigerland, as we rechristened ancient Devon, and, beating out into the Channel, turned the launch's nose southeast, to round Bolt Head and continue up the coast toward the Strait of Dover and the North Sea.

I was determined to reach London as soon as possible, that we might obtain fresh clothing, meet with cultured people, and learn from the lips of Englishmen the secret of the two centuries since the East had been divorced from the West.

Our first stopping place was the Isle of Wight. We entered the Solent about ten o'clock one morning, and I must confess that my heart sank as we came close to shore. No lighthouse was visible, though one was plainly indicated upon my map. Upon neither shore was sign of human habitation. We skirted the northern shore of the island in fruitless search for man, and then at last landed upon an eastern point, where Newport should have stood, but where only weeds and great trees and tangled wild wood rioted, and not a single man-made thing was visible to the eye.

Before landing, I had the men substitute soft bullets for the steel-jacketed projectiles with which their belts and magazines were filled. Thus equipped, we felt upon more even terms with the tigers; but there was no sign of the tigers, and I decided that they must be confined to the mainland.

After eating, we set out in search of fuel, leaving Taylor to guard the launch. For reason I could not trust Snider alone. I knew that he looked with disapproval upon my plan to visit England, and I did not know but what at his first opportunity he might desert us, taking the launch with him, and attempt to return to Pan-America.

That he would be fool enough to venture it I did not doubt.

We had gone inland for a mile or more, and were passing through a park-like wood, when we came suddenly upon the first human beings we had seen since we sighted the English coast.

There were a score of men in the party. Hairy, half-naked men they were, resting in the shade of a great tree. At the first sight of us they sprang to their feet with wild yells, seizing long spears that had lain beside them as they rested.

For a matter of fifty yards they ran from us as rapidly as they could, and then they turned and surveyed us for a moment. Evidently emboldened by the scarcity of our numbers, they commenced to advance upon us, brandishing their spears and shouting horribly.

They were short and muscular of build, with long hair and beards tangled and matted with filth. Their heads, however, were shapely, and their eyes, though fierce and warlike, were intelligent.

Appreciation of these physical attributes came later, of course, when I had better opportunity to study the men at close range and under circumstances less fraught with danger and excitement. At the moment I saw, and with unmixed wonder, only a score of wild savages charging down upon us, where I had expected to find a community of civilized and enlightened people.

Each of us was armed with rifle, revolver, and cutlass, but as we stood shoulder to shoulder facing the wild men I was loath to give the command to fire upon them, inflicting death or suffering upon strangers with whom we had no quarrel, and so I attempted to restrain them for the moment that we might parley with them.

To this end I raised my left hand above my head with the palm toward them as the most natural gesture indicative of peaceful intentions which occurred to me. At the same time I called aloud to them that we were friends, though, from their appearance, there was nothing to indicate that they might understand Pan-American, or ancient English, which are of course practically identical.

At my gesture and words they ceased their shouting and came to a halt a few paces from us. Then, in deep tones, one who was in advance of the others and whom I took to be the chief or leader of the party replied in a tongue which while intelligible to us, was so distorted from the English language from which it evidently had sprung that it was with difficulty that we interpreted it.

"Who are you," he asked, "and from what country?"

I told him that we were from Pan-America, but he only shook his head and asked where that was. He had never heard of it, or of the Atlantic Ocean which I told him separated his country from mine.

"It has been two hundred years," I told him, "since a Pan-American visited England."

"England?" he asked. "What is England?"

"Why this is a part of England!" I exclaimed.

"This is Grubitten," he assured me. "I know nothing about England, and I have lived here all my life."

It was not until long after that the derivation of Grubitten occurred to me. Unquestionably it is a corruption of Great Britain, a name formerly given to the large island comprising England, Scotland and Wales. Subsequently we heard it pronounced Grabritin and Grubritten.

I then asked the fellow if he could direct us to Ryde or Newport; but again he shook his head, and said that he never had heard of such countries. And when I asked him if there were any cities in this country he did not know what I meant, never having heard the word cities.

I explained my meaning as best I could by stating that by city I referred to a place where many people lived together in houses.

"Oh," he exclaimed, "you mean a camp! Yes, there are two great camps here, East Camp and West Camp. We are from East Camp."

The use of the word camp to describe a collection of habitations naturally suggested war to me, and my next question was as to whether the war was over, and who had been victorious.

"No," he replied to this question. "The war is not yet over; but it soon will be, and it will end, as it always does, with the Westenders running away—we, the Eastenders, are always victorious."

"No," I said, seeing that he referred to the petty tribal wars of his little island, "I mean the Great War, the war with Germany. Is it ended—and who was victorious?"

He shook his head impatiently.

"I never heard," he said, "of any of these strange countries of which you speak."

It seemed incredible, and yet it was true. These people living at the very seat of the Great War knew nothing of it, though but two centuries had passed since, to our knowledge, it had been running in the height of its titanic frightfulness all about them, and to us upon the far side of the Atlantic still was a subject of keen interest.

Here was a lifelong inhabitant of the Isle of Wight who never had heard of either Germany or England! I turned to him quite suddenly with a new question.

"What people live upon the mainland?" I asked, and pointed in the direction of the Hants coast.

"No one lives there," he replied.

"Long ago, it is said, my people dwelt across the waters upon that other land; but the wild beasts devoured them in such numbers that finally they were driven here, paddling across upon logs and driftwood, nor has any dared return since, because of the frightful creatures which dwell in that horrid country."

"Do no other peoples ever come to your country in ships?" I asked.

He never heard the word ship before, and did not know its meaning; but he assured me that until we came he had thought that there were no other peoples in the world other than the Grubittens, who consist of the Eastenders and the Westenders of the ancient Isle of Wight.

Assured that, we were inclined to friendliness, our new acquaintances led us to their village, or, as they call it, camp. There we found a thousand people, perhaps, dwelling in rude shelters, and living upon the fruits of the chase and such sea food as is obtainable close to shore, for they had no boats, nor any knowledge of such things.

Their weapons were most primitive, consisting of rude spears tipped with pieces of metal pounded roughly into shape. They had no literature, no religion, and recognized no law other than the law of might. They produce fire by striking a bit of flint and steel together, but for the most part they ate their food raw. Marriage is unknown among them, and while they have the word, mother, they did not know what I meant by "father". The males fight for the favor of the females. They practice infanticide, and kill the aged and the physically unfit.

The family consists of the mother and the children, the men dwelling sometimes in one hut and sometimes in another. Owing to their bloody duels, they are always numerically inferior to the women, so there is shelter for them all.

We spent several hours in the village, where we were objects of the greatest curiosity. The inhabitants examined our clothing and all our belongings, and asked innumerable questions concerning the strange country from which we had come and the manner of our coming.

I questioned many of them concerning past historical events; but they knew nothing beyond the narrow limits of their island and the savage, primitive life they led there. London they had never heard of, and they assured me that I would find no human beings upon the mainland.

Much saddened by what I had seen, I took my departure from them, and the three of us made our way back to the launch, accompanied by about five hundred men, women, girls, and boys.

As we sailed away, after procuring the necessary ingredients of our chemical fuel, the Grubittens lined the shore in silent wonder at the strange sight of our dainty craft dancing over the sparkling waters, and watched us until we were lost to their sight.

Chapter IV

It was during the morning of July 6, 2137, that we entered the mouth of the Thames—to the best of my knowledge the first Western keel to cut those historic waters for two hundred and twenty-one years!

But where were the tugs and the lighters and the barges, the lightships and the buoys, and all those countless attributes which went to make up the myriad life of the ancient Thames?

Gone! All gone! Only silence and desolation reigned where once the commerce of the world had centered.

I could not help but compare this once great waterway with the waters about our New York, or Rio, or San Diego, or Valparisso. They had become what they are today during the two centuries of the profound peace which we of the navy have been prone to deplore. And what, during this same period, had shorn the waters of the Thames of their pristine grandeur?

Militarist that I am, I could find but a single word of explanation—war!

I bowed my head and turned my eyes downward from the lonely and depressing sight, and in a silence which none of us seemed willing to break, we proceeded up the deserted river.

We had reached a point which, from my map, I imagined must have been about the former site of Erith, when I discovered a small band of antelope a short distance inland. As we were now entirely out of meat once more, and as I had given up all expectations of finding a city upon the site of ancient London, I determined to land and bag a couple of the animals.

Assured that they would be timid and easily frightened, I decided to stalk them alone, telling the men to wait at the boat until I called to them to come and carry the carcasses back to the shore.

Crawling carefully through the vegetation, making use of such trees and bushes as afforded shelter, I came at last almost within easy range of my quarry, when the antlered head of the buck went suddenly into the air, and then, as though in accordance with a prearranged signal, the whole band moved slowly off, farther inland.

As their pace was leisurely, I determined to follow them until I came again within range, as I was sure that they would stop and feed in a short time.

They must have led me a mile or more at least before they again halted and commenced to browse upon the rank, luxuriant grasses. All the time that I had followed them I had kept both eyes and ears alert for sign or sound that would indicate the presence of Felis tigris; but so far not the slightest indication of the beast had been apparent.

As I crept closer to the antelope, sure this time of a good shot at a large buck, I suddenly saw something that caused me to forget all about my prey in wonderment.

It was the figure of an immense grey-black creature, rearing its colossal shoulders twelve or fourteen feet above the ground. Never in my life had I seen such a beast, nor did I at first recognize it, so different in appearance is the live reality from the stuffed, unnatural specimens preserved to us in our museums.

But presently I guessed the identity of the mighty creature as Elphas africanus, or, as the ancient commonly described it, African elephant.

The antelope, although in plain view of the huge beast, paid not the slightest attention to it, and I was so wrapped up in watching the mighty pachyderm that I quite forgot to shoot at the buck and presently, and in quite a startling manner, it became impossible to do so.

The elephant was browsing upon the young and tender shoots of some low bushes, waving his great ears and switching his short tail. The antelope, scarce twenty paces from him, continued their feeding, when suddenly, from close beside the latter, there came a most terrifying roar, and I saw a great, tawny body shoot from the concealing verdure beyond the antelope full upon the back of a small buck.

Instantly the scene changed from one of quiet and peace to indescribable chaos. The startled and terrified buck uttered cries of agony. His fellows broke and leaped off in all directions. The elephant raised his trunk, and, trumpeting loudly, lumbered off through the wood, crushing down small trees and trampling bushes in his mad flight.

Growling horribly, a huge lion stood across the body of his prey—such a creature as no Pan-American of the twenty-second century had ever beheld until my eyes rested upon this lordly specimen of "the king of beasts." But what a different creature was this fierce-eyed demon, palpitating with life and vigor, glossy of coat, alert, growling magnificent, from the dingy, motheaten replicas beneath their glass cases in the stuffy halls of our public museums.

I had never hoped or expected to see a living lion, tiger, or elephant—using the common terms that were familiar to the ancients, since they seem to me less unwieldy than those now in general use among us—and so it was with sentiments not unmixed with awe that I stood gazing at this regal beast as, above the carcass of his kill, he roared out his challenge to the world.

So enthralled was I by the spectacle that I quite forgot myself, and the better to view him, the great lion, I had risen to my feet and stood, not fifty paces from him, in full view.

For a moment he did not see me, his attention being directed toward the retreating elephant, and I had ample time to feast my eyes upon his splendid proportions, his great head, and his thick black mane.

Ah, what thoughts passed through my mind in those brief moments as I stood there in rapt fascination! I had come to find a wondrous civilization, an instead I found a wild-beast monarch of the realm where English kings had ruled. A lion reigned, undisturbed, within a few miles of the seat of one of the greatest governments the world has ever known, his domain a howling wilderness, where yesterday fell the shadows of the largest city in the world.

It was appalling; but my reflections upon this depressing subject were doomed to sudden extinction—the lion had discovered me.

For an instant he stood silent and motionless as one of the mangy effigies at home; but only for an instant. Then, with a most ferocious roar, and without the slightest hesitancy or warning, he charged upon me.

He forsook the prey already dead beneath him for the pleasures of the delectable tidbit, man. From the remorselessness with which the great carnivora of modern England hunted man, I am constrained to believe that, whatever their appetites in times past, they have cultivated a gruesome taste for human flesh.

As I threw my rifle to my shoulder, I thanked God, the ancient God of my ancestors, that I had replaced the hard-jacketed bullets in my weapon with soft-nosed projectiles, for though this was my first experience with Felis leo, I knew the moment that I faced that charge that even my wonderfully perfected firearm would be as futile as a peashooter unless I chanced to place my first bullet in a vital spot.

Unless you had seen it you could not believe credible the speed of a charging lion. Apparently the animal is not built for speed, nor can he maintain it for long; but for a matter of forty or fifty yards there is, I believe, no animal on earth that can overtake him.

Like a bolt he bore down upon me; but, fortunately for me, I did not lose my head. I guessed that no bullet would kill him instantly. I doubted that I could pierce his skull. There was hope, though, in finding his heart through his exposed chest, or, better yet, of breaking his shoulder or foreleg, and bringing him up long enough to pump more bullets into him and finish him.

I covered his left shoulder and pulled the trigger as he was almost upon me. It stopped him. With a terrific howl of pain and rage, the brute rolled over and over upon the ground almost to my feet. As he came I pumped two more bullets into him, and as he struggled to rise, clawing viciously at me, I put a bullet in his spine.

That finished him, and I am free to admit that I was mighty glad of it. There was a great tree close behind me, and, stepping within its shade, I leaned against it, wiping the perspiration from my face, for the day was hot, and the exertion and excitement left me exhausted.

I stood there, resting, for a moment, preparatory to turning and retracing my steps to the launch, when, without warning, something whizzed through space straight toward me. There was a dull thud of impact as it struck the tree, and as I dodged to one side and turned to look at the thing I saw a heavy spear imbedded in the wood not three inches from where my head had been.

The thing had come from a little to one side of me, and, without waiting to investigate at the instant, I leaped behind the tree, and, circling it, peered around the other side to get a sight of my would-be murderer.

This time I was pitted against men—the spear told me that all too plainly—but so long as they didn't take me unawares or from behind I had little fear of them.

Cautiously I edged about the far side of the trees until I could obtain a view of the spot from which the spear must have come, and when I did I saw the head of a man just emerging from behind a bush.

The fellow was quite similar in type to those I had seen upon the Isle of Wight. He was hairy and unkempt, and as he finally stepped into view I saw that he was garbed in the same primitive fashion.

He stood for a moment gazing about in search of me, and then he advanced. As he did so a number of others, precisely like him, stepped from the concealing verdure of nearby bushes and followed in his wake. Keeping the tree between them and me, I ran back a short distance until I found a clump of underbrush that would effectually conceal me, for I wished to discover the strength of the party and its armament before attempting to parley with it.

The useless destruction of any of these poor creature was the farthest idea from my mind. I should have liked to have spoken with them; but I did not care to risk having to use my high-powered rifle upon them other than in the last extremity.

Once in my new place of concealment, I watched them as they approached the tree. There were about thirty men in the party and one woman—a girl whose hands seemed to be bound behind her and who was being pulled along by two of the men.

They came forward warily, peering cautiously into every bush and halting often. At the body of the lion, they paused, and I could see from their gesticulations and the higher pitch of their voices that they were much excited over my kill.

But presently they resumed their search for me, and as they advanced I became suddenly aware of the unnecessary brutality with which the girl's guards were treating her. She stumbled once, not far from my place of concealment, and after the balance of the party had passed me. As she did so one of the men at her side jerked her roughly to her feet and struck her across the mouth with his fist.

Instantly my blood boiled, and forgetting every consideration of caution, I leaped from my concealment, and, springing to the man's side, felled him with a blow.

So unexpected had been my act that it found him and his fellow unprepared; but instantly the latter drew the knife that protruded from his belt and lunged viciously at me, at the same time giving voice to a wild cry of alarm.

The girl shrank back at sight of me, her eyes wide in astonishment, and then my antagonist was upon me. I parried his first blow with my forearm, at the same time delivering a powerful blow to his jaw that sent him reeling back; but he was at me again in an instant, though in the brief interim I had time to draw my revolver.

I saw his companion crawling slowly to his feet, and the others of the party racing down upon me. There was no time to argue now, other than with the weapons we wore, and so, as the fellow lunged at me again with the wicked-looking knife, I covered his heart and pulled the trigger.

Without a sound, he slipped to the earth, and then I turned the weapon upon the other guard, who was now about to attack me. He, too, collapsed, and I was alone with the astonished girl.

The balance of the party was some twenty paces from us, but coming rapidly. I seized her arm and drew her after me behind a nearby tree, for I had seen that with both their comrades down the party were preparing to launch their spears.

With the girl safe behind the tree, I stepped out in sight of the advancing foe, shouting to them that I was no enemy, and that they should halt and listen to me; but for answer they only yelled in derision and launched a couple of spears at me, both of which missed.

I saw then that I must fight, yet still I hated to slay them, and it was only as a final resort that I dropped two of them with my rifle, bringing the others to a temporary halt. Again I appealed to them to desist; but they only mistook my solicitude for them for fear, and, with shouts of rage and derision, leaped forward once again to overwhelm me.

It was now quite evident that I must punish them severely, or, myself, die and relinquish the girl once more to her captors. Neither of these things had I the slightest notion of doing, and so I again stepped from behind the tree, and, with all the care and deliberation of target practice, I commenced picking off the foremost of my assailants.

One by one the wild men dropped, yet on came the others, fierce and vengeful, until, only a few remaining, these seemed to realize the futility of combating my modern weapon with their primitive spears, and, still howling wrathfully, withdrew toward the west.

Now, for the first time, I had an opportunity to turn my attention toward the girl, who had stood, silent and motionless, behind me as I pumped death into my enemies and hers from my automatic rifle.

She was of medium height, well formed, and with fine, clear-cut features. Her forehead was high, and her eyes both intelligent and beautiful. Exposure to the sun had browned a smooth and velvety skin to a shade which seemed to enhance rather than mar an altogether lovely picture of youthful femininity.

A trace of apprehension marked her expression—I cannot call it fear since I have learned to know her—and astonishment was still apparent in her eyes. She stood quite erect, her hands still bound behind her, and met my gaze with level, proud return.

"What language do you speak?" I asked. "Do you understand mine?"

"Yes," she replied; "it is similar to my own—I am Grabritin. What are you?"

"I am a Pan-American," I answered. She shook her head. "What is that?"

I pointed toward the west. "Far away, across the ocean."

Her expression altered a trifle. A slight frown contracted her brow. The expression of apprehension deepened.

"Take off your cap," she said, and when, to humor her strange request, I did as she bid, she appeared relieved. Then she edged to one side and leaned over seemingly to peer behind me. I turned quickly to see what she discovered, but finding nothing, wheeled about to see that her expression was once more altered.

"You are not from there?" and she pointed toward the east. It was a half question. "You are not from across the water there?"

"No," I assured her, "I am from Pan-America, far away to the west. Have you ever heard of Pan-America?"

She shook her head in negation. "I do not care where you are from," she explained, "if you are not from there, and I am sure you are not, for the men from there have horns and tails."

It was with difficulty that I restrained a smile.

"Who are the men from there?" I asked.

"They are bad men," she replied. "Some of my people do not believe that there are such creatures; but we have a legend—a very old, old legend, that once the men from there came across to Grabritin. They came upon the water, and under the water, and even in the air. They came in great numbers, so that they rolled across the land like a great gray fog. They brought with them thunder and lightning and smoke that killed, and they fell upon us and slew our people by the thousands and the hundreds of thousands; but at last we drove them back to the water's edge, back into the sea, where many were drowned. Some escaped, and these our people followed—men, women, and even children, we followed them back. That is all. The legend says our people never returned. Maybe they were all killed. Maybe they still are there. But this, also, is in the legend, that as we drove the men back across the water they swore that they would return, and that when they left our shores they would leave no human being alive behind them. I was afraid that you were from there."

"By what name were these men called?" I asked.

"We call them only the 'men from there,'" she replied, pointing toward the east. "I have never heard that they had another name."

In the light of what I knew of ancient history, it was not difficult for me to guess the nationality of those she described simply as "the men from over there". But what utter and appalling devastation the Great War must have wrought to have erased not only every sign of civilization from the face of this great land; but even the name of the enemy from the knowledge and language of the people.

I could only account for it on the hypothesis that the country had been entirely depopulated except for a few scattered and forgotten children, who, in some marvelous manner, had been preserved by Providence to repopulate the land. These children had, doubtless, been too young to retain in their memories to transmit to their children any but the vaguest suggestion of the cataclysm which had overwhelmed their parents.

Professor Cortoran, since my return to Pan-America, has suggested another theory which is not entirely without claim to serious consideration. He points out that it is quite beyond the pale of human instinct to desert little children as my theory suggests the ancient English must have done. He is more inclined to believe that the expulsion of the foe from England was synchronous with widespread victories by the allies upon the continent, and that the people of England merely emigrated from their ruined cities and their devastated, blood-drenched fields to the mainland, in the hope of finding in the domain of the conquered enemy cities and farms which should replace those they had lost.

The learned professor assumes that while a long-continued war had strengthened rather than weakened the instinct of paternal devotion, it had also dulled other humanitarian instincts, and raised to the first magnitude the law of the survival of the fittest, with the result that when the exodus took place the strong, the intelligent, and the cunning, together with their offspring, crossed the waters of the Channel or the North Sea to the continent, leaving in unhappy England only the helpless inmates of asylums for the feebleminded and insane.

My objection to this, that the present inhabitants of England are mentally fit, and could therefore, not have descended from an ancestry of undiluted lunacy he brushes aside with the assertion that insanity is not necessarily hereditary, and that even though it was, in many cases, a return to natural conditions from the state of high civilization which is thought to have induced mental disease in the ancient world would, after several generations, have thoroughly expunged every trade of the affliction from the brains and nerves of the descendants of the original maniacs.

Personally, I do not place much stock in Professor Cortoran's theory, though I admit that I am prejudiced. Naturally one does not care to believe that the object of his greatest affection is descended from a gibbering idiot and a raving maniac.

But I am forgetting the continuity of my narrative—a continuity which I desire to maintain, though I fear that I shall often be led astray, so numerous and varied are the bypaths of speculation which lead from the present day story of the Grabritins into the mysterious past of their forbears.

As I stood talking with the girl I presently recollected that she still was bound, and with a word of apology I drew my knife and cut the rawhide thongs which confined her wrists at her back.

She thanked me, and with such a sweet smile that I should have been amply repaid by it for a much more arduous service.

"And now," I said, "let me accompany you to your home and see you safely again under the protection of your friends."

"No," she said, with a hint of alarm in her voice; "you must not come with me—Buckingham will kill you."

Buckingham. The name was famous in ancient English history. Its survival, with many other illustrious names, is one of the strongest arguments in refutal of Professor Cortoran's theory; yet it opens no new doors to the past, and, on the whole, rather adds to than dissipates the mystery.

"And who is Buckingham," I asked, "and why should he wish to kill me?"

"He would think that you had stolen me," she replied, "and as he wishes me for himself, he will kill any other whom he thinks desires me. He killed Wettin a few days ago. My mother told me once that Wettin was my father. He was king. Now Buckingham is king."

Here, evidently, were a people slightly superior to those of the Isle of Wight. These must have at least the rudiments of civilized government since they recognized one among them as ruler, with the title king. Also, they retained the word father. The girl's pronunciation, while far from identical with ours, was much closer than the tortured dialect of the Eastenders of the Isle of Wight. The longer I talked with her the more hopeful I became of finding here, among her people, some records, or traditions, which might assist in clearing up the historic enigma of the past two centuries. I asked her if we were far from the city of London; but she did not know what I meant. When I tried to explain, describing mighty buildings of stone and brick, broad avenues, parks, palaces, and countless people she but shook her head sadly.

"There is no such place near by," she said. "Only the Camp of the Lions has places of stone where the beasts lair; but there are no people in the Camp of the Lions. Who would dare go there!" And she shuddered.

"The Camp of the Lions," I repeated. "And where is that, and what?"

"It is there," she said, pointing up the river toward the west. "I have seen it from a great distance, but I have never been there. We are much afraid of the lions, for this is their country, and they are angry that man has come to live here.

"Far away there," and she pointed toward the southwest, "is the land of tigers, which is even worse than this, the land of the lions, for the tigers are more numerous than the lions and hungrier for human flesh. There were tigers here long ago, but both the lions and the men set upon them and drove them off."

"Where did these savage beasts come from?" I asked.

"Oh," she replied, "they have been here always—it is their country."

"Do they not kill and eat your people?" I asked.

"Often, when we meet them by accident, and we are too few to slay them, or when one goes too close to their camp; but seldom do they hunt us, for they find what food they need among the deer and wild cattle, and, too, we make them gifts, for are we not intruders in their country? Really we live upon good terms with them, though I should not care to meet one were there not many spears in my party."

"I should like to visit this Camp of the Lions," I said.

"Oh, no, you must not!" cried the girl. "That would be terrible. They would eat you." For a moment, then, she seemed lost in thought; but presently she turned upon me with: "You must go now, for any minute Buckingham may come in search of me. Long since should they have learned that I am gone from the camp—they watch over me very closely—and they will set out after me. Go! I shall wait here until they come in search of me."

"No," I told her. "I'll not leave you alone in a land infested by lions and other wild beasts. If you won't let me go as far as your camp with you, then I'll wait here until they come in search of you."

"Please go!" she begged. "You have saved me, and I would save you: but nothing will save you if Buckingham gets his hands on you. He is a bad man. He wishes to have me for his woman so that he may be king. He would kill anyone who befriended me, for fear that I might become another's."

"Didn't you say that Buckingham is already the king?" I asked.

"He is. He took my mother for his woman after he had killed Wettin; but my mother will die soon—she is very old—and then the man to whom I belong will become king."

Finally, after much questioning, I got the thing through my head. It appears that the line of descent is through the women. A man is merely head of his wife's family—that is all. If she chances to be the oldest female member of the "royal" house, he is king. Very naively the girl explained that there was seldom any doubt as to who a child's mother was.

This accounted for the girl's importance in the community and for Buckingham's anxiety to claim her, though she told me that she did not wish to become his woman, for he was a bad man and would make a bad king. But he was powerful, and there was no other man who dared dispute his wishes.

"Why not come with me," I suggested, "if you do not wish to become Buckingham's?"

"Where would you take me?" she asked.

Where, indeed! I had not thought of that; but before I could reply to her question she shook her head and said: "No, I cannot leave my people. I must stay and do my best, even if Buckingham gets me; but you must go at once. Do not wait until it is too late. The lions have had no offering for a long time, and Buckingham would seize upon the first stranger as a gift to them."

I did not perfectly understand what she meant, and was about to ask her when a heavy body leaped upon me from behind, and great arms encircled my neck. I struggled to free myself and turn upon my antagonist, but in another instant I was overwhelmed by a half dozen powerful, half-naked men, while a score of others surrounded me, a couple of whom seized the girl.

I fought as best I could for my liberty and for hers, but the weight of numbers was too great, though I had the satisfaction at least of giving them a good fight.

When they had overpowered me, and I stood, my hands bound behind me, at the girl's side, she gazed commiseratingly at me.

"It is too bad that you did not do as I bid you," she said, "for now it has happened just as I feared—Buckingham has you."

"Which is Buckingham?" I asked.

"I am Buckingham," growled a burly, unwashed brute, swaggering truculently before me. "And who are you who would have stolen my woman?"

The girl spoke up then and tried to explain that I had not stolen her; but on the contrary I had saved her from the men from the "Elephant Country" who were carrying her away.

Buckingham only sneered at her explanation, and a moment later gave the command that started us all off toward the west. We marched for a matter of an hour or so, coming at last to a collection of rude huts, fashioned from branches of trees covered with skins and grasses and sometimes plastered with mud. All about the camp they had erected a wall of saplings pointed at the tops and fire hardened.

This palisade was a protection against both man and beasts, and within it dwelt upward of two thousand persons, the shelters being built very close together, and sometimes partially underground, like deep trenches, with the poles and hides above merely as protection from the sun and rain.

The older part of the camp consisted almost wholly of trenches, as though this had been the original form of dwellings which was slowly giving way to the drier and airier surface domiciles. In these trench habitations I saw a survival of the military trenches which formed so famous a part of the operations of the warring nations during the twentieth century.

The women wore a single light deerskin about their hips, for it was summer, and quite warm. The men, too, were clothed in a single garment, usually the pelt of some beast of prey. The hair of both men and women was confined by a rawhide thong passing about the forehead and tied behind. In this leathern band was stuck feathers, flowers, or the tails of small mammals. All wore necklaces of the teeth or claws of wild beasts, and there were numerous metal wristlets and anklets among them.

They wore, in fact, every indication of a most primitive people—a race which had not yet risen to the heights of agriculture or even the possession of domestic animals. They were hunters—the lowest plane in the evolution of the human race of which science takes cognizance.

And yet as I looked at their well shaped heads, their handsome features, and their intelligent eyes, it was difficult to believe that I was not among my own. It was only when I took into consideration their mode of living, their scant apparel, the lack of every least luxury among them, that I was forced to admit that they were, in truth, but ignorant savages.

Buckingham had relieved me of my weapons, though he had not the slightest idea of their purpose or uses, and when we reached the camp he exhibited both me and my arms with every indication of pride in this great capture.

The inhabitants flocked around me, examining my clothing, and exclaiming in wonderment at each new discovery of button, buckle, pocket, and flap. It seemed incredible that such a thing could be, almost within a stone's throw of the spot where but a brief two centuries before had stood the greatest city of the world.

They bound me to a small tree that grew in the middle of one of their crooked streets; but the girl they released as soon as we had entered the enclosure. The people greeted her with every mark of respect as she hastened to a large hut near the center of the camp.

Presently she returned with a fine looking, white-haired woman, who proved to be her mother. The older woman carried herself with a regal dignity that seemed quite remarkable in a place of such primitive squalor.

The people fell aside as she approached, making a wide way for her and her daughter. When they had come near and stopped before me the older woman addressed me.

"My daughter has told me," she said, "of the manner in which you rescued her from the men of the elephant country. If Wettin lived you would be well treated; but Buckingham has taken me now, and is king. You can hope for nothing from such a beast as Buckingham."

The fact that Buckingham stood within a pace of us and was an interested listener appeared not to temper her expressions in the slightest.

"Buckingham is a pig," she continued. "He is a coward. He came upon Wettin from behind and ran his spear through him. He will not be king for long. Some one will make a face at him, and he will run away and jump into the river."

The people began to titter and clap their hands. Buckingham became red in the face. It was evident that he was far from popular.

"If he dared," went on the old lady, "he would kill me now; but he does not dare. He is too great a coward. If I could help you I should gladly do so; but I am only queen—the vehicle that has helped carry down, unsullied, the royal blood from the days when Grabritin was a mighty country."

The old queen's words had a noticeable effect upon the mob of curious savages which surrounded me. The moment they discovered that the old queen was friendly to me and that I had rescued her daughter they commenced to accord me a more friendly interest, and I heard many words spoken in my behalf, and demands were made that I not be harmed.

But now Buckingham interfered. He had no intention of being robbed of his prey. Blustering and storming, he ordered the people back to their huts, at the same time directing two of his warriors to confine me in a dugout in one of the trenches close to his own shelter.

Here they threw me upon the ground, binding my ankles together and trussing them up to my wrists behind. There they left me, lying upon my stomach—a most uncomfortable and strained position, to which was added the pain where the cords cut into my flesh.

Just a few days ago my mind had been filled with the anticipation of the friendly welcome I should find among the cultured Englishmen of London. Today I should be sitting in the place of honor at the banquet board of one of London's most exclusive clubs, feted and lionized.

The actuality! Here I lay, bound hand and foot, doubtless almost upon the very site of a part of ancient London, yet all about me was a primeval wilderness, and I was a captive of half-naked wild men.

I wondered what had become of Delcarte and Taylor and Snider. Would they search for me? They could never find me, I feared, yet if they did, what could they accomplish against this horde of savage warriors?

Would that I could warn them. I thought of the girl—doubtless she could get word to them; but how was I to communicate with her? Would she come to see me before I was killed? It seemed incredible that she should not make some slight attempt to befriend me; yet, as I recalled, she had made no effort to speak with me after we had reached the village—she had hastened to her mother the moment she had been liberated. Though she had returned with the old queen, she had not spoken to me, even then. I began to have my doubts.

Finally I came to the conclusion that I was absolutely friendless except for the old queen. For some unaccountable reason my rage against the girl for her ingratitude rose to colossal proportions.

For a long time I waited for some one to come to my prison whom I might ask to bear word to the queen; but I seemed to have been forgotten. The strained position in which I lay became unbearable. I wriggled and twisted until I managed to turn myself partially upon my side, where I lay half facing the entrance to the dugout.

Presently my attention was attracted by the shadow of something moving in the trench without, and a moment later the figure of a child appeared, creeping upon all fours, as, wide-eyed, and prompted by childish curiosity, a little girl crawled to the entrance of my hut and peered cautiously and fearfully in.

I did not speak at first for fear of frightening the little one away; but when I was satisfied that her eyes had become sufficiently accustomed to the subdued light of the interior, I smiled.

Instantly the expression of fear faded from her eyes to be replaced with an answering smile. "Who are you little girl?" I asked.

"My name is Mary," she replied. "I am Victory's sister."

"And who is Victory?"

"You do not know who Victory is?" she asked, in astonishment.

I shook my head in negation.

"You saved her from the elephant country people, and yet you say you do not know her!" she exclaimed.

"Oh, so she is Victory, and you are her sister! I have not heard her name before—that is why I did not know whom you meant," I explained. Here was just the messenger for me. Fate was becoming more kind.

"Will you do something for me, Mary?" I asked.

"If I can."

"Go to your mother, the queen, and ask her to come to me," I said. "I have a favor to ask."

She said that she would, and with a parting smile she left me.

For what seemed many hours I awaited her return, chafing with impatience. The afternoon wore on and night came, and yet no one came near me. My captors brought me neither food or water. I was suffering considerable pain where the rawhide thongs cut into my swollen flesh. I thought that they had either forgotten me, or that it was their intention to leave me here to die of starvation.

Once I heard a great uproar in the village. Men were shouting—women were screaming and moaning. After a time this subsided, and again there was a long interval of silence.

Half the night must have been spent when I heard a sound in the trench near the hut—it resembled muffled sobs. Presently a figure appeared, silhouetted against the lesser darkness beyond the doorway. It crept inside the hut.

"Are you here?" whispered a childlike voice.

It was Mary! She had returned. The thongs no longer hurt me—the pangs of hunger and thirst disappeared. I realized that it had been loneliness from which I suffered most.

"Mary!" I exclaimed. "You are a good girl. You have come back, after all—I had commenced to think that you would not. Did you give my message to the queen? Will she come? Where is she?"

The child's sobs increased, and she flung herself upon the dirt floor of the hut, apparently overcome by grief.

"What is it?" I asked. "Why do you cry?"

"The queen, my mother, will not come to you," she said, between sobs. "She is dead. Buckingham has killed her. Now he will take Victory, for Victory is queen. He kept us fastened up in our shelter, for fear that Victory would escape him; but I dug a hole beneath the back wall and got out. I came to you, because you saved Victory once before, and I thought that you might save her again, and me, also. Tell me that you will."

"I am bound and helpless, Mary," I replied. "Otherwise I would do what I could to save you and your sister."

"I will set you free!" cried the girl, creeping to my side. "I will set you free, and then you may come and slay Buckingham."

"Gladly!" I assented.

"We must hurry," she went on, as she fumbled with the hard knots in the stiffened rawhide, "for Buckingham will be after you soon. He must make an offering to the lions at dawn before he can take Victory—the taking of a queen requires a human offering!"

"And I am to be the offering?" I asked.

"Yes," she said, tugging at a knot. "Buckingham has been wanting a sacrifice ever since he killed Wettin, that he might slay my mother and take Victory."

The thought was horrible, not solely because of the hideous fate to which I was condemned; but from the contemplation it engendered of the sad decadence of a once enlightened race. To these depths of ignorance, brutality, and superstition had the vaunted civilization of twentieth-century England been plunged, and by what? War! I felt the structure of our time-honored militaristic arguments crumbling about me.

Mary labored with the thongs that confined me. They proved refractory—defying her tender, childish fingers. She assured me, however, that she would release me, if "they" did not come too soon.

But, alas, they came. We heard them coming down the trench, and I bade Mary hide in a corner, lest she be discovered and punished. There was naught else she could do, and so she crawled away into the Stygian blackness behind me.

Presently two warriors entered. The leader exhibited a unique method of discovering my whereabouts in the darkness. He advanced slowly, kicking out viciously before him. Finally he kicked me in the face—then he knew where I was.

A moment later I had been jerked roughly to my feet. One of the fellows stopped and severed the bonds that held my ankles. I could scarcely stand alone. The two pulled and hauled me through the low doorway and along the trench. A party of forty or fifty warriors were awaiting us at the brink of the excavation some hundred yards from the hut.

Hands were lowered to us, and we were dragged to the surface. Then commenced a long march. We stumbled through the underbrush wet with dew, our way lighted by a score of torchbearers who surrounded us; but the torches were not to light the way—that was but incidental. They were carried to keep off the huge carnivora that moaned and coughed and roared about us.

The noises were hideous. The whole country seemed alive with lions. Yellow-green eyes blazed wickedly at us from out the surrounding darkness. My escort carried long, heavy spears. These they kept ever pointed toward the beast of prey, and I learned from snatches of the conversation I overheard that occasionally there might be a lion who would brave even the terrors of fire to leap in upon human prey—it was for such that the spears were always couched.

But nothing of the sort occurred during this hideous death march, and with the first pale heralding of dawn we reached our goal—an open place in the midst of a tangled wildwood. Here rose in crumbling grandeur the first evidences I had seen of the ancient civilization which once had graced fair Albion—a single, time-worn arch of masonry.

"The entrance to the Camp of the Lions!" murmured one of the party in a voice husky with awe.

Here the party knelt, while Buckingham recited a weird, prayer-like chant. It was rather long, and I recall only a portion of it, which ran, if my memory serves me, somewhat as follows:

"Lord of Grabritin, we
Fall on our knees to thee,
This gift to bring.
Greatest of kings art thou!
To thee we humbly bow!
Peace to our camp allow.
God save thee, king!

Then the party rose, and dragging me to the crumbling arch, made me fast to a huge, corroded, copper ring which was dangling from an eyebolt imbedded in the masonry.

None of them, not even Buckingham, seemed to feel any personal animosity toward me. They were naturally rough and brutal, as primitive men are supposed to have been since the dawn of humanity; but they did not go out of their way to maltreat me.

With the coming of dawn the number of lions about us seemed to have greatly diminished—at least they made less noise—and as Buckingham and his party disappeared into the woods, leaving me alone to my terrible fate, I could hear the grumblings and growlings of the beasts diminishing with the sound of the chant, which the party still continued. It appeared that the lions had failed to note that I had been left for their breakfast, and had followed off after their worshippers instead.

But I knew the reprieve would be but for a short time, and though I had no wish to die, I must confess that I rather wished the ordeal over and the peace of oblivion upon me.

The voices of the men and the lions receded in the distance, until finally quiet reigned about me, broken only by the sweet voices of birds and the singing of the summer wind in the trees.

It seemed impossible to believe that in this peaceful woodland setting the frightful thing was to occur which must come with the passing of the next lion who chanced within sight or smell of the crumbling arch.

I strove to tear myself loose from my bonds; but succeeded only in tightening them about my arms. Then I remained passive for a long time, letting the scenes of my lifetime pass in review before my mind's eye.

I tried to imagine the astonishment, incredulity, and horror with which my family and friends would be overwhelmed if, for an instant, space could be annihilated and they could see me at the gates of London.

The gates of London! Where was the multitude hurrying to the marts of trade after a night of pleasure or rest? Where was the clang of tramcar gongs, the screech of motor horns, the vast murmur of a dense throng?

Where were they? And as I asked the question a lone, gaunt lion strode from the tangled jungle upon the far side of the clearing. Majestically and noiselessly upon his padded feet the king of beasts moved slowly toward the gates of London and toward me.

Was I afraid? I fear that I was almost afraid. I know that I thought that fear was coming to me, and so I straightened up and squared my shoulders and looked the lion straight in the eyes—and waited.

It is not a nice way to die—alone, with one's hands fast bound, beneath the fangs and talons of a beast of prey. No, it is not a nice way to die, nor a pretty way.

The lion was halfway across the clearing when I heard a slight sound behind me. The great cat stopped in his tracks. He lashed his tail against his sides now, instead of simply twitching its tip, and his low moan became a thunderous roar.

As I craned my neck to catch a glimpse of the thing that had aroused the fury of the beast before me, it sprang through the arched gateway and was at my side—with parted lips and heaving bosom and disheveled hair—a bronzed and lovely vision to eyes that had never harbored hope of rescue.

It was Victory, and in her arms she clutched my rifle and revolver. A long knife was in the doeskin belt that supported the doeskin skirt tightly about her lithe limbs. She dropped my weapons at my feet, and, snatching the knife from its resting place, severed the bonds that held me. I was free, and the lion was preparing to charge.

"Run!" I cried to the girl, as I bent and seized my rifle; but she only stood there at my side, her bared blade ready in her hand.

The lion was bounding toward us now in prodigous leaps. I raised the rifle and fired. It was a lucky shot, for I had no time to aim carefully, and when the beast crumpled and rolled, lifeless, to the ground, I went upon my knees and gave thanks to the God of my ancestors.

And, still upon my knees, I turned, and taking the girl's hand in mine, I kissed it. She smiled at that, and laid her other hand upon my head.

"You have strange customs in your country," she said.

I could not but smile at that when I thought how strange it would seem to my countrymen could they but see me kneeling there on the site of London, kissing the hand of England's queen.

"And now," I said, as I rose, "you must return to the safety of your camp. I will go with you until you are near enough to continue alone in safety—then I shall try to return to my comrades."

"I will not return to the camp," she replied.

"But what shall you do?" I asked.

"I do not know—only I shall never go back while Buckingham lives. I should rather die than go back to him. Mary came to me, after they had taken you from the camp, and told me. I found your strange weapons and followed with them. It took me a little longer, for often I had to hide in the trees that the lions might not get me; but I came in time, and now you are free to go back to your friends."

"And leave you here?" I exclaimed.

She nodded, but I could see through all her brave front that she was frightened at that thought. I could not leave her, of course; but what in the world I was to do, cumbered with the care of a young woman, and a queen at that, I was at a loss to know. I pointed out that phase of it to her; but she only shrugged her shapely shoulders and pointed to her knife.

It was evident that she felt entirely competent to protect herself.

As we stood there we heard the sound of voices. They were coming from the forest through which we had passed when we had come from camp.

"They are searching for me," said the girl. "Where shall we hide?"

I didn't relish hiding; but when I thought of the innumerable dangers which surrounded us and the comparatively small amount of ammunition that I had with me, I hesitated to provoke a battle with Buckingham and his warriors when, by flight, I could avoid them and preserve my cartridges against emergencies which could not be escaped.

"Would they follow us there?" I asked, pointing through the archway into the Camp of the Lions.

"Never," she replied, "for, in the first place, they would know that we would not dare go there, and in the second they themselves would not dare."

"Then we shall take refuge in the Camp of the Lions," I said.

She shuddered and drew closer to me.

"You dare?" she asked.

"Why not?" I returned. "We shall be safe from Buckingham, and you have seen, for the second time in two days, that lions are harmless before my weapons. Then, too, I can find my friends easiest in this direction, for the River Thames runs through this place you call the Camp of the Lions, and it is farther down the Thames that my friends are awaiting me. Do you not dare come with me?"

"I dare follow wherever you lead," she answered simply.

And so I turned and passed beneath the great arch into the city of London.

Chapter V

As we entered deeper into what had once been the city, the evidences of man's past occupancy became more frequent. For a mile from the arch there was only a riot of weeds and undergrowth and trees covering small mounds and little hillocks that, I was sure, were formed of the ruins of stately buildings of the dead past.

But presently we came upon a district where shattered walls still raised their crumbling tops in sad silence above the grass-grown sepulchers of their fallen fellows. Softened and mellowed by ancient ivy stood these sentinels of sorrow, their scarred faces still revealing the rents and gashes of shrapnel and of bomb.

Contrary to our expectations, we found little indication that lions in any great numbers laired in this part of ancient London. Well-worn pathways, molded by padded paws, led through the cavernous windows or doorways of a few of the ruins we passed, and once we saw the savage face of a great, black-maned lion scowling down upon us from a shattered stone balcony.

We followed down the bank of the Thames after we came upon it. I was anxious to look with my own eyes upon the famous bridge, and I guessed, too, that the river would lead me into that part of London where stood Westminster Abbey and the Tower.

Realizing that the section through which we had been passing was doubtless outlying, and therefore not so built up with large structures as the more centrally located part of the old town, I felt sure that farther down the river I should find the ruins larger. The bridge would be there in part, at least, and so would remain the walls of many of the great edifices of the past. There would be no such complete ruin of large structures as I had seen among the smaller buildings.

But when I had come to that part of the city which I judged to have contained the relics I sought I found havoc that had been wrought there even greater than elsewhere.

At one point upon the bosom of the Thames there rises a few feet above the water a single, disintegrating mound of masonry. Opposite it, upon either bank of the river, are tumbled piles of ruins overgrown with vegetation.

These, I am forced to believe, are all that remain of London Bridge, for nowhere else along the river is there any other slightest sign of pier or abutment.

Rounding the base of a large pile of grass-covered debris, we came suddenly upon the best preserved ruin we had yet discovered. The entire lower story and a part of the second story of what must once have been a splendid public building rose from a great knoll of shrubbery and trees, while ivy, thick and luxuriant, clambered upward to a summit of the broken walls.

In many places the gray stone was still exposed, its smoothly chiseled face pitted with the scars of battle. The massive portal yawned, somber and sorrowful, before us, giving a glimpse of marble halls within.

The temptation to enter was too great. I wished to explore the interior of this one remaining monument of civilization now dead beyond recall. Through this same portal, within these very marble halls, had Gray and Chamberlin and Kitchener and Shaw, perhaps, come and gone with the other great ones of the past.

I took Victory's hand in mine.

"Come!" I said. "I do not know the name by which this great pile was known, nor the purposes it fulfilled. It may have been the palace of your sires, Victory. From some great throne within your forebears may have directed the destinies of half the world. Come!"

I must confess to a feeling of awe as we entered the rotunda of the great building. Pieces of massive furniture of another day still stood where man had placed them centuries ago. They were littered with dust and broken stone and plaster; but, otherwise, so perfect was their preservation I could hardly believe that two centuries had rolled by since human eyes were last set upon them.

Through one great room after another we wandered, hand in hand, while Victory asked many questions and for the first time I began to realize something of the magnificence and power of the race from whose loins she had sprung.

Splendid tapestries, now mildewed and rotting, hung upon the walls. There were mural paintings, too, depicting great historic events of the past. For the first time Victory saw the likeness of a horse, and she was much affected by a huge oil which depicted some ancient cavalry charge against a battery of field guns.

In other pictures there were steamships, battleships, submarines, and quaint looking railway trains—all small and antiquated in appearance to me, but wonderful to Victory. She told me that she would like to remain for the rest of her life where she could look at those pictures daily.

From room to room we passed until presently we emerged into a mighty chamber, dark and gloomy, for its high and narrow windows were choked and clogged by ivy. Along one panel wall we groped, our eyes slowly becoming accustomed to the darkness. A rank and pungent odor pervaded the atmosphere.

We had made our way about half the distance across one end of the great apartment when a low growl from the far end brought us to a startled halt.

Straining my eyes through the gloom, I made out a raised dais at the extreme opposite end of the hall. Upon the dais stood two great chairs, highbacked and with great arms.

The throne of England! But what were those strange forms about it?

Victory gave my hand a quick, excited little squeeze.

"The lions!" she whispered.

Yes, lions indeed! Sprawled about the dais were a dozen huge forms, while upon the seat of one of the thrones a small cub lay curled in slumber.

As we stood there for a moment, spellbound by the sight of those fearsome creatures occupying the very thrones of the sovereigns of England, the low growl was repeated, and a great male rose slowly to his feet.

His devilish eyes bored straight through the semidarkness toward us. He had discovered the interloper. What right had man within this palace of the beasts? Again he opened his giant jaws, and this time there rumbled forth a warning roar.

Instantly eight or ten of the other beasts leaped to their feet. Already the great fellow who had spied us was advancing slowly in our direction. I held my rifle ready; but how futile it appeared in the face of this savage horde.

The foremost beast broke into a slow trot, and at his heels came the others. All were roaring now, and the din of their great voices reverberating through the halls and corridors of the palace formed the most frightful chorus of thunderous savagery imaginable to the mind of man.

And then the leader charged, and upon the hideous pandemonium broke the sharp crack of my rifle, once, twice, thrice. Three lions rolled, struggling and biting, to the floor. Victory seized my arm, with a quick: "This way! Here is a door," and a moment later we were in a tiny ante-chamber at the foot of a narrow stone staircase.

Up this we backed, Victory just behind me, as the first of the remaining lions leaped from the throne room and sprang for the stairs. Again I fired; but others of the ferocious beasts leaped over their fallen fellows and pursued us.

The stairs were very narrow—that was all that saved us—for as I backed slowly upward, but a single lion could attack me at a time, and the carcasses of those I slew impeded the rushes of the others.

At last we reached the top. There was a long corridor from which opened many doorways. One, directly behind us, was tight closed. If we could open it and pass into the chamber behind we might find a respite from attack.

The remaining lions were roaring horribly. I saw one sneaking very slowly up the stairs toward us.

"Try that door," I called to Victory. "See if it will open."

She ran up to it and pushed.

"Turn the knob!" I cried, seeing that she did not know how to open a door; but neither did she know what I meant by knob.

I put a bullet in the spine of the approaching lion and leaped to Victory's side. The door resisted my first efforts to swing it inward. Rusted hinges and swollen wood held it tightly closed; but at last it gave, and just as another lion mounted to the top of the stairway it swung in, and I pushed Victory across the threshold.

Then I turned to meet the renewed attack of the savage foe. One lion fell in his tracks, another stumbled to my very feet, and then I leaped within and slammed the portal to.

A quick glance showed me that this was the only door to the small apartment in which we had found sanctuary, and, with a sigh of relief, I leaned for a moment against the panels of the stout barrier that separated us from the ramping demons without.

Across the room, between two windows, stood a flat-topped desk. A little pile of white and brown lay upon it close to the opposite edge. After a moment of rest I crossed the room to investigate. The white was the bleached human bones—the skull, collar bones, arms, and a few of the upper ribs of a man. The brown was the dust of a decayed military cap and blouse. In a chair before the desk were other bones, while more still strewed the floor beneath the desk and about the chair. A man had died sitting there with his face buried in his arms—two hundred years ago.

Beneath the desk were a pair of spurred military boots, green and rotten with decay. In them were the leg bones of a man. Among the tiny bones of the hands was an ancient fountain pen, as good, apparently, as the day it was made, and a metal covered memoranda book, closed over the bones of an index finger.

It was a gruesome sight—a pitiful sight—this lone inhabitant of mighty London.

I picked up the metal covered memoranda book. Its pages were rotten and stuck together. Only here and there was a sentence or a part of a sentence legible. The first that I could read was near the middle of the little volume:

"His majesty left for Tunbridge Wells today, he . . . jesty was stricken . . . terday. God give she does not die . . . am military governor of Lon . . ."

And farther on:

"It is awful . . . hundred deaths today . . . worse than the bombardm . . ."

Nearer the end I picked out the following:

"I promised his maj . . . . e will find me here when he ret . . . . alone."

The most legible passage was on the next page:

"Thank God we drove them out. There is not a single . . . man on British soil today; but at what awful cost. I tried to persuade Sir Phillip to urge the people to remain; but they are mad with fear of the Death, and rage at our enemies. He tells me that the coast cities are packed . . . waiting to be taken across. What will become of England, with none left to rebuild her shattered cities!"

And the last entry:

" . . . . alone. Only the wild beasts . . . A lion is roaring now beneath the palace windows. I think the people feared the beasts even more than they did the Death. But they are gone, all gone, and to what? How much better conditions will they find on the continent? All gone—only I remain. I promised his majesty, and when he returns he will find that I was true to my trust; for I shall be awaiting him. God save the King!"

That was all. This brave and forever nameless officer died nobly at his post—true to his country and his king. It was the Death, no doubt, that took him.

Some of the entries had been dated. From the few legible letters and figures which remained I judge the end came some time in August, 1937; but of that I am not at all certain.

The diary has cleared up at least one mystery that had puzzled me not a little, and now I am surprised that I had not guessed its solution myself—the presence of African and Asiatic beasts in England.

Acclimated by years of confinement in the zoological gardens, they were fitted to resume in England the wild existence for which nature had intended them, and once free, had evidently bred prolifically, in marked contrast to the captive exotics of twentieth century Pan-America, which had gradually become fewer until extinction occurred some time during the twenty-first century.

The Palace, if such it was, lay not far from the banks of the Thames.

The room in which we were imprisoned overlooked the river, and I determined the attempt to escape in this direction.

To descend through the palace was out of the question; but outside we could discover no lions. The stems of the ivy which clambered upward past the window of the room were as large around as my arm. I knew that they would support our weight, and as we could gain nothing by remaining longer in the palace, I decided to descend by way of the ivy and follow along down the river in the direction of the launch.

Naturally I was much handicapped by the presence of the girl; but I could not abandon her, though I had no idea what I should do with her after rejoining my companions. That she would prove a burden and an embarrassment I was certain, but she had made it equally plain to me that she would never return to her people to mate with Buckingham.

I owed my life to her, and, all other considerations aside, that was sufficient demand upon my gratitude and my honor to necessitate my suffering every inconvenience in her service. Too, she was queen of England; but, by far the most potent argument in her favor, she was a woman in distress—and a young and very beautiful one.

And so, though I wished a thousand times that she was back in her camp, I never let her guess it; but did all that lay within my power to serve and protect her. I thank God now that I did so.

With the lions still padding back and forth beyond the closed door, Victory and I crossed the room to one of the windows. I had outlined my plan to her, and she had assured me that she could descend the ivy without assistance. In fact she smiled a trifle at my question.

Swinging myself outward, I began the descent, and had come to within a few feet of the ground, being just opposite a narrow window, when I was startled by a savage growl almost in my ear, and then a great taloned paw darted from the aperture to seize me, and I saw the snarling face of a lion within the embrasure.

Releasing my hold upon the ivy, I dropped the remaining distance to the ground, saved from laceration only because the lion's paw struck the thick stem of ivy.

The creature was making a frightful racket now, leaping back and forth from the floor to the broad window ledge, tearing at the masonry with his claws in vain attempts to reach me; but the opening was too narrow, and the masonry too solid.

Victory had commenced the descent, but I called to her to stop just above the window, and, as the lion reappeared, growling and snarling, I put a .33 bullet in his face, and at the same moment Victory slipped quickly past him, dropping into my upraised arms that were awaiting her.

The roaring of the beasts that had discovered us, together with the report of my rifle, had set the balance of the fierce inmates of the palace into the most frightful uproar I have ever heard.

I feared that it would not be long before intelligence or instinct would draw them from the interiors and set them upon our trail, the river, nor had we much more than reached it when a lion bounded around the corner of the edifice we had just quitted and stood looking about as though in search of us.

Following, came others, while Victory and I crouched in hiding behind a clump of bushes close to the bank of the river. The beasts sniffed about the ground for a while, but they did not chance to go near the spot where we had stood beneath the window that had given us escape.

Presently a black-maned male raised his head, and, with cocked ears and glaring eyes, glazed straight at the bush behind which we lay. I could have sworn that he had discovered us, and when he took a few short and stately steps in our direction I raised my rifle and covered him; but after a long, tense moment he looked away, and turned to glare in another direction.

I breathed a sigh of relief, and so did Victory—I could feel her body quiver as she lay pressed close to me, our cheeks almost touching as we both peered through the same small opening in the foliage.

I turned to give her a reassuring smile as the lion indicated that he had not seen us, and as I did so she, too, turned her face toward mine, for the same purpose, doubtless. Anyway, as our heads turned simultaneously, our lips brushed together. A startled expression came into Victory's eyes as she drew back in evident confusion.

As for me, the strangest sensation that I have ever experienced claimed me for an instant. A peculiar, tingling thrill ran through my veins, and my head swam. I could not account for it.

Naturally, being a naval officer and consequently in the best society of the federation, I have seen much of women. With others, I have laughed at the assertions of the savants that modern man is a cold and passionless creation in comparison with the males of former ages—in a word, that love, as the one grand passion, had ceased to exist.

I do not know, now, but that they were more nearly right than we have guessed, at least in so far as modern civilized woman is concerned. I have kissed many women—young and beautiful and middle aged and old, and many that I had no business kissing—but never before had I experienced that remarkable and altogether delightful thrill that followed the accidental brushing of my lips against the lips of Victory.

The occurrence interested me, and I was tempted to experiment further; but when I would have essayed it another new and entirely unaccountable force restrained me—for the first time in my life I felt embarrassment in the presence of a woman.

What further might have developed I cannot say, for at that moment a perfect she-devil of a lioness, with keener eyes than her lord and master, discovered us. She came trotting toward our place of concealment, growling and baring her yellow fangs.

I waited for an instant, hoping that I might be mistaken, and that she would turn off in some other direction; but no—she increased her trot to a gallop, and then I fired at her; but the bullet, though it struck her full in the breast, didn't stop her.

Screaming with pain and rage, the creature fairly flew toward us. Behind her came other lions. Our case looked hopeless. We were upon the brink of the river. There seemed no avenue of escape, and I knew that even my modern automatic rifle was inadequate in the face of so many of these fierce beasts.

To remain where we were would have been suicidal. We were both standing now, Victory keeping her place bravely at my side, when I reached the only decision open to me.

Seizing the girl's hand, I turned, just as the lioness crashed into the opposite side of the bushes, and, dragging Victory after me, leaped over the edge of the bank into the river.

I did not know that lions are not fond of water, nor did I know if Victory could swim; but death, immediate and terrible, stared us in the face if we remained, and so I took the chance.

At this point the current ran close to the shore, so that we were immediately in deep water, and, to my intense satisfaction, Victory struck out with a strong, overhand stroke and set all my fears on her account at rest.

But my relief was short-lived. That lioness, as I have said before, was a veritable devil. She stood for a moment glaring at us, then like a shot she sprang into the river and swam swiftly after us.

Victory was a length ahead of me.

"Swim for the other shore!" I called to her.

I was much impeded by my rifle, having to swim with one hand while I clung to my precious weapon with the other. The girl had seen the lioness take to the water, and she had also seen that I was swimming much more slowly than she, and what did she do? She started to drop back to my side.

"Go on!" I cried. "Make for the other shore, and then follow down until you find my friends. Tell them that I sent you, and with orders that they are to protect you. Go on! Go on!"

But she only waited until we were again swimming side by side, and I saw that she had drawn her long knife, and was holding it between her teeth.

"Do as I tell you!" I said to her sharply; but she shook her head.

The lioness was overhauling us rapidly. She was swimming silently, her chin just touching the water; but blood was streaming from between her lips. It was evident that her lungs were pierced.

She was almost upon me. I saw that in a moment she would take me under her forepaws, or seize me in those great jaws. I felt that my time had come; but I meant to die fighting, and so I turned, and, treading water, raised my rifle above my head and awaited her.

Victory, animated by a bravery no less ferocious than that of the dumb beast assailing us, swam straight for me. It all happened so swiftly that I cannot recall the details of the kaleidoscopic action which ensued. I knew that I rose high out of the water, and, with clubbed rifle, dealt the animal a terrific blow upon the skull; that I saw Victory, her long blade flashing in her hand, close, striking, upon the beast; that a great paw fell upon my shoulder, and that I was swept beneath the surface of the water like a straw before the prow of a freighter.

Still clinging to my rifle, I rose again, to see the lioness struggling in her death throes but an arm's length from me. Scarcely had I risen than the beast turned upon her side, struggled frantically for an instant, and then sank.

Chapter VI

Victory was nowhere in sight. Alone, I floated upon the bosom of the Thames. In that brief instant I believe that I suffered more mental anguish than I have crowded into all the balance of my life before or since. A few hours before, I had been wishing that I might be rid of her, and now that she was gone I would have given my life to have her back again.

Wearily I turned to swim about the spot where she had disappeared, hoping that she might rise once at least, and I would be given the opportunity to save her; and, as I turned, the water boiled before my face and her head shot up before me. I was on the point of striking out to seize her, when a happy smile illumined her features.

"You are not dead!" she cried. "I have been searching the bottom for you. I was sure that the blow she gave you must have disabled you," and she glanced about for the lioness.

"She has gone?" she asked.

"Dead," I replied.

"The blow you struck her with the thing you call rifle stunned her," she explained, "and then I swam in close enough to get my knife into her heart."

Ah, such a girl! I could not but wonder what one of our own Pan-American women would have done under like circumstances; but then, of course, they have not been trained by stern necessity to cope with the emergencies and dangers of savage primeval life.

Along the bank we had just quitted a score of lions paced to and fro, growling menacingly. We could not return, and we struck out for the opposite shore. I am a strong swimmer, and had no doubt as to my ability to cross the river; but I was not so sure about Victory, so I swam close behind her, to be ready to give her assistance should she need it.

She did not, however, reaching the opposite bank as fresh, apparently, as when she entered the water. Victory is a wonder. Each day that we were together brought new proofs of it. Nor was it her courage or vitality only which amazed me. She had a head on those shapely shoulders of hers, and dignity! My, but she could be regal when she chose!

She told me that the lions were fewer upon this side of the river; but that there were many wolves, running in great packs later in the year. Now they were north somewhere, and we should have little to fear from them, though we might meet with a few.

My first concern was to take my weapons apart and dry them, which was rather difficult in the face of the fact that every rag about me was drenched; but finally, thanks to the sun and much rubbing, I succeeded, though I had no oil to lubricate them.

We ate some wild berries and roots that Victory found, and then we set off again down the river, keeping an eye open for game on one side and the launch on the other, for I thought that Delcarte, who would be the natural leader during my absence, might run up the Thames in search of me.

The balance of that day we sought in vain for game or for the launch, and when night came we lay down, our stomachs empty, to sleep beneath the stars. We were entirely unprotected from attack from wild beasts, and for this reason I remained awake most of the night, on guard; but nothing approached us, though I could hear the lions roaring across the river, and once I thought I heard the howl of a beast to the north of us—it might have been a wolf.

Altogether, it was a most unpleasant night, and I determined then that if we were forced to sleep out again that I should provide some sort of shelter which would protect us from attack while we slept.

Toward morning I dozed, and the sun was well up when Victory aroused me by gently shaking my shoulder.

"Antelope!" she whispered in my ear; and, as I raised my head, she pointed upriver. Crawling to my knees, I looked in the direction she indicated, to see a buck standing upon a little knoll some two hundred yards from us. There was good cover between the animal and me, and so, though I might have hit him at two hundred yards, I preferred to crawl closer to him and make sure of the meat we both so craved.

I had covered about fifty yards of the distance, and the beast was still feeding peacefully, so I thought that I would make even surer of a hit by going ahead another fifty yards, when the animal suddenly raised his head and looked away upriver. His whole attitude proclaimed that he was startled by something beyond him that I could not see.

Realizing that he might break and run and that I should then probably miss him entirely, I raised my rifle to my shoulder; but even as I did so the animal leaped into the air, and simultaneously there was a sound of a shot from beyond the knoll.

For an instant I was dumbfounded. Had the report come from downriver, I should have instantly thought that one of my own men had fired; but coming from upriver it puzzled me considerably. Who could there be with firearms in primitive England other than we of the *Coldwater*?

Victory was directly behind me, and I motioned for her to lie down, as I did, behind the bush from which I had been upon the point of firing at the antelope. We could see that the buck was quite dead, and from our hiding place we waited to discover the identity of his slayer when the latter should approach and claim his kill.

We had not long to wait, and when I saw the head and shoulders of a man appear above the crest of the knoll, I sprang to my feet, with a heartfelt cry of joy, for it was Delcarte.

At the sound of my voice, Delcarte half raised his rifle in readiness for the attack of an enemy; but a moment later he recognized me, and was coming rapidly to meet us. Behind him was Snider. They both were astounded to see me upon the north bank of the river, and much more so at the sight of my companion.

Then I introduced them to Victory, and told them that she was queen of England. They thought, at first, that I was joking; but when I had recounted my adventures and they realized that I was in earnest they believed me.

They told me that they had followed me inshore when I had not returned from the hunt; that they had met the men of the elephant country, and had had a short and one-sided battle with the fellows, and that afterward they had returned to the launch with a prisoner, from whom they had learned that I had probably been captured by the men of the lion country.

With the prisoner as a guide they had set off upriver in search of me, but had been much delayed by motor trouble, and had finally camped after dark a half mile above the spot where Victory and I had spent the night—they must have passed us in the dark, and why I did not hear the sound of the propeller I do not know, unless it passed me at a time when the lions were making an unusually ear-splitting din upon the opposite side.

Taking the antelope with us, we all returned to the launch, where we found Taylor as delighted to see me alive again as Delcarte had been. I cannot say truthfully that Snider evinced much enthusiasm at my rescue.

Taylor had found the ingredients for chemical fuel, and the distilling of them had, with the motor trouble, accounted for their delay in setting out after me.

The prisoner that Delcarte and Snider had taken was a powerful young fellow, from the elephant country. Notwithstanding the fact that they had all assured him to the contrary, he still could not believe that we would not kill him.

He assured us that his name was Thirty-Six, and, as he could not count above ten, I am sure that he had no conception of the correct meaning of the word, and that it may have been handed down to him either from the military number of an ancestor who had served in the English ranks during the Great War, or that originally it was the number of some famous regiment with which a forbear fought.

Now that we were reunited, we held a council to determine what course we should pursue in the immediate future. Snider was still for setting out to sea and returning to Pan-America, but the better judgment of Delcarte and Taylor ridiculed the suggestion—we should not have lived a fortnight.

To remain in England, constantly menaced by wild beasts and men equally as wild, seemed about as bad. I suggested that we cross the channel and ascertain if we could not discover a more enlightened and civilized people upon the continent. I was sure that some trace of the ancient culture and greatness of Europe must remain. Germany, probably, would be much as it was during the twentieth century, for, in common with most Pan-Americans, I was positive that Germany had been victorious in the Great War.

But Snider demurred at the suggestion. He said that it was bad enough to have come this far—he did not want to make it worse by going to the continent. The outcome of it was that I finally lost my patience, and told him that from then on he would do what I thought best—that I purposed to assume command of the party, and that they might all consider themselves under my orders, as much so as though we were still aboard the *Coldwater* and in Pan-American waters.

Delcarte and Taylor immediately assured me that they had not for an instant assumed anything different, and that they were as ready to follow and obey me here as they would be upon the other side of /3/0.

Snider said nothing; but he wore a sullen scowl, and I wished then, as I had before and as I did to a much greater extent later, that fate had not decreed that he should have chanced to be a member of the launch's party upon that memorable day when last we quitted the *Coldwater*.

Victory, who was given a voice in our councils, was all for going to the continent, or anywhere else, in fact, where she might see new sights and experience new adventures.

"Afterward we can come back to Grabritin," she said, "and if Buckingham is not dead and we can catch him away from his men and kill him, then I can return to my people, and we can all live in peace and happiness."

She spoke of killing Buckingham with no greater concern than one might evince in the contemplated destruction of a sheep; yet she was neither cruel nor vindicative. In fact, Victory is a very sweet and womanly woman; but human life is of small account beyond /3/0—a legacy from the bloody days when thousands of men perished in the trenches between the rising and the setting of a sun; when they laid them lengthwise in these same trenches and sprinkled dirt over them; when the Germans cored their corpses like wood and set fire to them; when women and children and old men were butchered; and great passenger ships torpedoed without warning.

Thirty-six, finally assured that we did not intend slaying him, was as keen to accompany us as was Victory.

The crossing to the continent was uneventful; its monotony being relieved, however, by the childish delight of Victory and Thirty-six in the novel experience of riding safely upon the bosom of the water, and of being so far from land.

With the possible exception of Snider, the little party appeared in the best of spirits, laughing and joking, or interestedly discussing the possibilities which the future held for us, what we should find upon the continent, and whether the inhabitants would be civilized or barbarian peoples.

Victory asked me to explain the difference between the two, and when I had tried to do so as clearly as possible, she broke into a gay little laugh.

"Oh," she cried, "then I am a barbarian!"

I could not but laugh, too, as I admitted that she was, indeed, a barbarian. She was not offended, taking the matter as a huge joke; but some time thereafter she sat in silence, apparently deep in thought. Finally she looked up at me, her strong white teeth gleaming behind her smiling lips.

"Should you take that thing you call 'razor'" she said, "and cut the hair from the face of Thirty-six, and exchange garments with him, you would be the barbarian and Thirty-six the civilized man. There is no other difference between you, except your weapons. Cloth you in a wolfskin, give you a knife and a spear, and set you down in the woods of Grabritin—of what service would your civilization be to you?"

Delcarte and Taylor smiled at her reply, but Thirty-six and Snider laughed uproariously. I was not surprised at Thirty-six, but I thought that Snider laughed louder than the occasion warranted. As a matter of fact, Snider, it seemed to me, was taking advantage of every opportunity, however slight, to show insubordination, and I determined then that at the first real breach of discipline I should take action that would remind Snider, even after, that I was still his commanding officer.

I could not help but notice that his eyes were much upon Victory, and I did not like it, for I knew the type of man he was; but as it would not be necessary ever to leave the girl alone with him I felt no apprehension for her safety.

After the incident of the discussion of barbarians I thought that Victory's manner toward me changed perceptibly. She held aloof from me, and when Snider took his turn at the wheel, sat beside him, upon the pretext that she wished to learn how to steer the launch. I wondered if she had guessed the man's antipathy for me, and was seeking his company solely for the purpose of piquing me.

Snider was, too, taking full advantage of his opportunity. Often he leaned toward the girl to whisper in her ear, and he laughed much, which was unusual with Snider.

Of course, it was nothing at all to me; yet, for some unaccountable reason, the sight of the two of them sitting there so close to one another and seeming to be enjoying each other's society to such a degree irritated me tremendously, and put me in such a bad humor that I took no pleasure whatsoever in the last few hours of the crossing.

We aimed to land near the site of ancient Ostend; but when we neared the coast we discovered no indication of any human habitations whatever, let alone a city. After we had landed, we found the same howling wilderness about us that we had discovered on the British Isle—there was no slightest indication that civilized man had ever set a foot upon that portion of the continent of Europe.

Although I had feared as much, since our experience in England, I could not but own to a feeling of marked disappointment, and to the gravest fears of the future, which induced a mental depression that was in no way dissipated by the continued familiarity between Victory and Snider.

I was angry with myself that I permitted that matter to affect me as it had. I did not wish to admit to myself that I was angry with this uncultured little savage—that it made the slightest difference to me what she did, or what she did not do—or that I could so lower myself as to feel personal enmity toward a common sailor; and yet, to be honest, I was doing both.

Finding nothing to detain us about the spot where Ostend once had stood, we set out up the coast in search of the mouth of the River Rhine, which I purposed ascending in search of civilized man. It was my intention to explore the Rhine as far up as the launch would take us. If we found no civilization there we would return to the North Sea, continue up the coast to the Elbe, and follow that river and the canals of Berlin. Here, at least, I was sure that we should find what we sought; and, if not, then all Europe had reverted to barbarism.

The weather remained fine, and we made excellent progress, but everywhere along the Rhine we met with the same disappointment—no sign of civilized man; in fact, no sign of man at all.

I was not enjoying the exploration of modern Europe as I had anticipated—I was unhappy. Victory seemed changed, too. I had enjoyed her company at first; but since the trip across the Channel I had held aloof from her.

Her chin was in the air most of the time, and yet I rather think that she regretted her friendliness with Snider, for I noticed that she avoided him entirely. He, on the contrary, emboldened by her former friendliness, sought every opportunity to be near her. I should have liked nothing better than a reasonably good excuse to punch his head; yet, paradoxically, I was ashamed of myself for harboring him any ill will. I realized that there was something the matter with me; but I did not know what it was.

Matters remained thus for several days, and we continued our journey up the Rhine. At Cologne, I had hoped to find some reassuring indications; but there was no Cologne, and as there had been no other cities along the river up to that point, the devastation was infinitely greater than time alone could have wrought. Great guns, bombs, and mines must have leveled every building that man had raised, and then nature, unhindered, had covered the ghastly evidence of human depravity with her beauteous mantle of verdure. Splendid trees reared their stately tops where splendid cathedrals once had reared their domes, and sweet wild flowers blossomed in simple serenity in soil that once was drenched with human blood.

Nature had reclaimed what man had once stolen from her and defiled. A herd of zebras grazed where once the German kaiser may have reviewed his troops. An antelope rested peacefully in a bed of daisies where, perhaps, two hundred years ago a big gun belched its terror-laden messages of death, of hate, of destruction against the works of man and God alike.

We were in need of fresh meat, yet I hesitated to shatter the quiet and peaceful serenity of the view with the crack of a rifle and the death of one of those beautiful creatures before us. But it must be done—we must eat. I left the work to Delcarte, however, and in a moment we had two antelope and the landscape to ourselves.

After eating, we boarded the launch and continued up the river. For two days we passed through a primeval wilderness, unrelieved. In the afternoon of the second day we landed upon the west bank of the river, and, leaving Snider and Thirty-six to guard Victory and the launch, Delcarte, Taylor, and I set out after game.

We tramped away from the river for upwards of an hour before discovering anything, and then only a small red deer, which Taylor brought down with a neat shot of two hundred yards. It was getting too late to proceed farther, so we rigged a sling, and the two men carried the deer back toward the launch while I walked a hundred yards ahead, in the hope of bagging something further for our larder.

We had covered about half the distance to the river, when I suddenly came face to face with a man. He was primitive and uncouth in appearance as the Grabritins—a shaggy, unkempt savage, clothed in a shirt of skin cured with the head on, the latter surmounting his own head to form a bonnet, and giving to him a most fearful and ferocious aspect.

The fellow was armed with a long spear and a club, the latter dangling down his back from a leathern thong about his neck. His feet were incased in hide sandals.

At sight of me, he halted for an instant, then turned and dove into the forest, and, though I called reassuringly to him in English he did not return nor did I again see him.

The sight of the wild man raised my hopes once more that elsewhere we might find men in higher state of civilization—it was the society of civilized man that I craved—and so, with a lighter heart, I continued on toward the river and the launch.

I was still some distance ahead of Delcarte and Taylor when I came in sight of the Rhine again; but I came to the water's edge before I noticed that anything was amiss with the party we had left there a few hours before.

My first intimation of disaster was the absence of the launch from its former moorings; and then, a moment later, I discovered the body of a man lying upon the bank. Running toward it, I saw that it was Thirty-six, and as I stopped and raised the Grabritin's head in my arms I heard a faint moan break from his lips. He was not dead; but that he was badly injured was all too evident.

Delcarte and Taylor came up a moment later, and the three of us worked over the fellow, hoping to revive him that he might tell us what had happened, and what had become of the others. My first thought was prompted by the sight I had recently had of the savage native. The little party had evidently been surprised, and in the attack Thirty-six had been wounded and the others taken prisoners. The thought was almost like a physical blow in the face—it stunned me. Victory in the hands of these abysmal brutes! It was frightful. I almost shook poor Thirty-six in my efforts to revive him.

I explained my theory to the others, and then Delcarte shattered it by a single movement of a hand—he drew aside the lion's skin that covered half of the Grabritin's breast, revealing a neat, round hole in Thirty-six's chest—a hole that could have been made by no other weapon than a rifle.

"Snider!" I exclaimed. Delcarte nodded. At about the same time the eyelids of the wounded man fluttered, and raised. He looked up at us, and very slowly the light of consciousness returned to his eyes.

"What happened, Thirty-six?" I asked him.

He tried to reply, but the effort caused him to cough, bringing about a hemorrhage of the lungs and again he fell back exhausted. For several long minutes he lay as one dead, then in an almost inaudible whisper he spoke.

"Snider—." He paused, tried to speak again, raised a hand, and pointed downriver. "They—went—back," and then he shuddered convulsively and died.

None of us voiced his belief; but I think they were all alike: Victory and Snider had stolen the launch, and deserted us.

Chapter VII

We stood there, grouped about the body of the dead Grabritin, looking futilely down the river to where it made an abrupt curve to the west a quarter of a mile below us, and was lost to sight, as though we expected to see the truant returning to us with our precious launch—the thing that meant life or death to us in this unfriendly, savage world.

I felt, rather than saw, Taylor turn his eyes slowly toward my profile, and, as mine swung to meet them, the expression upon his face recalled me to my duty and responsibility as an officer.

The utter hopelessness that was reflected in his face must have been the counterpart of what I myself felt; but in that brief instant I determined to hide my own misgivings that I might bolster up the courage of the others.

"We are lost!" was written as plainly upon Taylor's face as though his features were the printed words upon an open book. He was thinking of the launch, and of the launch alone. Was I? I tried to think that I was; but a greater grief than the loss of the launch could have engendered in me filled my heart—a sullen, gnawing misery which I tried to deny—which I refused to admit—but which persisted in obsessing me until my heart rose and filled my throat, and I could not speak when I would have uttered words of reassurance to my companions.

And then rage came to my relief—rage against he vile traitor who had deserted three of his fellow countrymen in so frightful a position. I tried to feel an equal rage against the woman; but somehow I could not, and kept searching for excuses for her—her youth, her inexperience, her savagery.

My rising anger swept away my temporary helplessness. I smiled, and told Taylor not to look so glum.

"We will follow them," I said, "and the chances are that we shall overtake them. They will not travel as rapidly as Snider probably hopes. He will be forced to halt for fuel and for food, and the launch must follow the windings of the river; we can take short cuts while they are traversing the detour. I have my map—thank God! I always carry it upon my person—and with that and the compass we will have an advantage over them."

My words seemed to cheer them both, and they were for starting off at once in pursuit. There was no reason why we should delay, and we set forth down the river. As we tramped along, we discussed a question that was uppermost in the mind of each—what we should do with Snider when we had captured him, for with the action of pursuit had come the optimistic conviction that we should succeed. As a matter of fact, we had to succeed. The very thought of remaining in this utter wilderness for the rest of our lives was impossible.

We arrived at nothing very definite in the matter of Snider's punishment, since Taylor was for shooting him, Delcarte insisting upon that he should be hanged, while I, although fully conscious of the gravity of his offense, could not bring myself to giving the death penalty.

I fell to wondering what charm Victory had found in such a man as Snider, and why I insisted upon finding excuses for her and trying to defend her indefensible act. She was nothing to me. Aside from the natural gratitude I felt for her since she had saved my life, I owed her nothing. She was a half-naked little savage—I a gentleman, and an officer in the world's greatest navy. There could be no close bonds of interest between us.

This line of reflection I discovered to be as distressing as the former; but, though I tried to turn my mind to other things, it persisted in returning to the vision of an oval face, sun-tanned; of smiling lips, revealing white and even teeth; of brave eyes that harbored no shadow of guile; and of a tumbling mass of wavy hair that crowned the loveliest picture on which my eyes had ever rested.

Every time this vision presented itself I felt myself turn cold with rage and hate against Snider. I could forgive the launch; but if he had wronged her he should die—he should die at my own hands; in this I was determined.

For two days we followed the river northward, cutting off where we could, but confined for the most part to the game trails that paralleled the stream. One afternoon, we cut across a narrow neck of land that saved us many miles, where the river wound to the west and back again.

Here we decided to halt, for we had had a hard day of it, and, if the truth were known, I think that we had all given up hope of overtaking the launch other than by the merest accident.

We had shot a deer just before our halt, and, as Taylor and Delcarte were preparing it, I walked down to the water to fill our canteens. I had just finished, and was straightening up, when something floating around a bend above me caught my eye. For a moment I could not believe the testimony of my own senses. It was a boat.

I shouted to Delcarte and Taylor, who came running to my side.

"The launch!" cried Delcarte; and, indeed, it was the launch, floating downriver from above us. Where had it been? How had we passed it? And how were we to reach it now, should Snider and the girl discover us?

"It's drifting," said Taylor. "I see no one in it."

I was stripping off my clothes, and Delcarte soon followed my example. I told Taylor to remain on shore with the clothing and rifles. He might also serve us better there, since it would give him an opportunity to take a shot at Snider should the man discover us and show himself.

With powerful strokes we swam out in the path of the oncoming launch. Being a stronger swimmer than Delcarte, I soon was far in the lead, reaching the center of the channel just as the launch bore down upon me. It was drifting broadside on. I seized the gunwale and raised myself quickly, so that my chin topped the side. I expected a blow the moment that I came within the view of the occupants; but no blow fell.

Snider lay upon his back in the bottom of the boat alone. Even before I had clambered in and stooped above him I knew that he was dead. Without examining him further, I ran forward to the control board and pressed the starting button. To my relief, the mechanism responded—

the launch was uninjured. Coming about, I picked up Delcarte. He was astounded at the sight that met his eyes, and immediately fell to examining Snider's body for signs of life or an explanation of the manner in which he met his death.

The fellow had been dead for hours—he was cold and still; but Delcarte's search was not without results, for above Snider's heart was a wound, a slit about an inch in length—such a slit as a sharp knife would make, and in the dead fingers of one hand was clutched a strand of long brown hair—Victory's hair was brown.

They say that dead men tell no tales; but Snider told the story of his end as clearly as though the dead lips had parted and poured forth the truth. The beast had attacked the girl, and she had defended her honor.

We buried Snider beside the Rhine, and no stone marks his last resting place. Beasts do not require headstones.

Then we set out in the launch, turning her nose upstream. When I had told Delcarte and Taylor that I intended searching for the girl, neither had demurred.

"We had her wrong in our thoughts," said Delcarte, "and the least that we can do in expiation is to find and rescue her."

We called her name aloud every few minutes as we motored up the river; but, though we returned all the way to our former camping place, we did not find her. I then decided to retrace our journey, letting Taylor handle the launch, while Delcarte and I, upon opposite sides of the river, searched for some sign of the spot where Victory had landed.

We found nothing until we had reached a point a few miles above the spot where I had first seen the launch drifting down toward us, and there I discovered the remnants of a recent camp fire.

That Victory carried flint and steel I was aware, and that it was she who built the fire I was positive; but which way had she gone since she stopped here?

Would she go on down the river, that she might thus bring herself nearer her own Grabritin, or would she have sought to search for us upstream, where she had seen us last?

I had hailed Taylor, and sent him across the river to take in Delcarte, that the two might join me and discuss my discovery and our future plans.

While waiting for them, I stood looking out over the river, my back toward the woods that stretched away to the east behind me. Delcarte was just stepping into the launch upon the opposite side of the stream, when, without the least warning, I was violently seized by both arms and about the waist—three or four men were upon me at once; my rifle was snatched from my hands and my revolver from my belt.

I struggled for an instant; but finding my efforts of no avail, I ceased them, and turned my head to have a look at my assailants. At the same time several others of them walked around in front of me, and, to my astonishment, I found myself looking upon uniformed soldiery, armed with rifles, revolvers, and sabers, but with faces as black as coal.

Chapter VIII

Delcarte and Taylor were now in midstream, coming toward us, and I called to them to keep aloof until I knew whether the intentions of my captors were friendly or otherwise. My good men wanted to come on and annihilate the blacks; but there were upward of a hundred of the latter, all well armed, and so I commanded Delcarte to keep out of harm's way, and stay where he was till I needed him.

A young officer called and beckoned to them; but they refused to come, and so he gave orders that resulted in my hands being secured at my back, after which the company marched away, straight toward the east.

I noticed that the men wore spurs, which seemed strange to me; but when, late in the afternoon, we arrived at their encampment, I discovered that my captors were cavalrymen.

In the center of a plain stood a log fort, with blockhouses at each of its four corners. As we approached, I saw a herd of cavalry horses grazing under guard outside the walls of the post. They were small, stocky horses; but the telltale saddle galls proclaimed their calling. The flag flying from a tall staff inside the palisade was one which I had never before seen or heard of.

We marched directly into the compound, where the company was dismissed, with the exception of a guard of four privates, who escorted me in the wake of the young officer. The latter led us across a small parade ground, where a battery of light field guns was parked, and toward a log building, in front of which rose the flagstaff.

I was escorted within the building into the presence of an old negro, a fine looking man, with a dignified and military bearing. He was a colonel, I was to learn later, and to him I owe the very humane treatment that was accorded me while I remained his prisoner.

He listened to the report of his junior, and then turned to question me; but with no better results than the former had accomplished. Then he summoned an orderly, and gave some instructions. The soldier saluted, and left the room, returning in about five minutes with a hairy old white man—just such a savage, primeval-looking fellow as I had discovered in the woods the day that Snider had disappeared with the launch.

The colonel evidently expected to use the fellow as interpreter; but when the savage addressed me it was in a language as foreign to me as was that of the blacks. At last the old officer gave it up, and, shaking his head, gave instructions for my removal.

From his office I was led to a guardhouse, in which I found about fifty half-naked whites, clad in the skins of wild beasts. I tried to converse with them, but not one of them could understand Pan-American, nor could I make head or tall of their jargon.

For over a month I remained a prisoner there, working from morning until night at odd jobs about the headquarters building of the commanding officer. The other prisoners worked harder than I did, and I owe my better treatment solely to the kindliness and discrimination of the old colonel.

What had become of Victory, a Delcarte, of Taylor I could not know; nor did it seem likely that I should ever learn. I was most depressed; but I whiled away my time in performing the duties given me to the best of my ability and attempting to learn the language of my captors.

Who they were or where they came from was a mystery to me. That they were the outpost of some powerful black nation seemed likely, yet where the seat of that nation lay I could not guess.

They looked upon the whites as their inferiors, and treated us accordingly. They had a literature of their own, and many of the men, even the common soldiers, were omnivorous readers. Every two weeks a dust-covered trooper would trot his jaded mount into the post and deliver a bulging sack of mail at headquarters. The next day he would be away again upon a fresh horse toward the south, carrying the soldiers' letters to friends in that far off land of mystery from whence they all had come.

Troops, sometimes mounted and sometimes afoot, left the post daily for what I assumed to be patrol duty. I judged the little force of a thousand men were detailed here to maintain the authority of a distant government in a conquered country. Later, I learned that my surmise was correct, and this was but one of a great chain of similar posts that dotted the new frontier of the black nation into whose hands I had fallen.

Slowly I learned their tongue, so that I could understand what was said before me, and make myself understood. I had seen from the first that I was being treated as a slave—that all whites that fell into the hands of the blacks were thus treated.

Almost daily new prisoners were brought in, and about three weeks after I was brought in to the post a troop of cavalry came from the south to relieve one of the troops stationed there. There was great jubilation in the encampment after the arrival of the newcomers, old friendships were renewed and new ones made; but the happiest men were those of the troop that was to be relieved.

The next morning they started away, and as they were forced upon the parade ground we prisoners were marched from our quarters and lined up before them. A couple of long chains were brought, with rings in the links every few feet. At first I could not guess the purpose of these chains; but I was soon to learn.

A couple of soldiers snapped the first ring around the neck of a powerful white slave, and one by one the rest of us were herded to our places, and the work of shackling us neck to neck commenced.

The colonel stood watching the procedure. Presently his eyes fell upon me, and he spoke to a young officer at his side. The latter stepped toward me and motioned me to follow him. I did so, and was led back to the colonel.

By this time I could understand a few words of their strange language, and when the colonel asked me if I would prefer to remain at the post as his body servant, I signified my willingness as emphatically as possible, for I had seen enough of the brutality of the common soldiers toward their white slaves to have no desire to start out upon a march of unknown length, chained by the neck, and driven on by the great whips that a score of the soldiers carried to accelerate the speed of their charges.

About three hundred prisoners who had been housed in six prisons at the post marched out of the gates that morning, toward what fate and what future I could not guess. Neither had the poor devils themselves more than the most vague conception of what lay in store for them, except that they were going elsewhere to continue in the slavery that they had known since their capture by their black conquerors—a slavery that was to continue until death released them.

My position was altered at the post. From working about the headquarters office, I was transferred to the colonel's living quarters. I had greater freedom, and no longer slept in one of the prisons, but had a little room to myself off the kitchen of the colonel's log house.

My master was always kind to me, and under him I rapidly learned the language of my captors, and much concerning them that had been a mystery to me before. His name was Abu Belik. He was a colonel in the cavalry of Abysinns, a country of which I do not remember ever hearing, but which Colonel Belik assured me is the oldest civilized country in the world.

Colonel Belik was born in Adis Abeba, the capital of the empire, and until recently had been in command of the emperor's palace guard. Jealousy and the ambition and intrigue of another officer had lost him the favor of his emperor, and he had been detailed to this frontier post as a mark of his sovereign's displeasure.

Some fifty years before, the young emperor, Menelek XIV, was ambitious. He knew that a great world lay across the waters far to the north of his capitol. Once he had crossed the desert and looked out upon the blue sea that was the norther boundary of his dominions.

There lay another world to conquer. Menelek busied himself with the building of a great fleet, though his people were not a maritime race. His army crossed into Europe. It met with little resistance, and for fifty years his soldiers had been pushing his boundaries farther and farther toward the north.

"The yellow men from the east and north are contesting our rights here now," said the colonel; "but we shall win—we shall conquer the world, carrying Christianity to all the benighted heathen of Europe, and Asia as well."

"You are a Christian people?" I asked.

He looked at me in surprise, nodding his head affirmatively.

"I am a Christian," I said. "My people are the most powerful on earth."

He smiled, and shook his head indulgently, as a father to a child who sets up his childish judgment against that of his elders.

Then I set out to prove my point. I told him of our cities, of our army, of our great navy. He came right back at me asking for figures, and when he was done I had to admit that only in our navy were we numerically superior.

Menelek XIV is the undisputed rule of all the continent of Africa; of all of ancient Europe except the British Isles, Scandinavia, and eastern Russia; and has large possessions and prosperous colonies in what once were Arabia and Turkey in Asia.

He has a standing army of ten million men, and his people possess slaves—white slaves—to the number of ten or fifteen million.

Colonel Belik was much surprised, however, upon his part, to learn of the great nation which lay across the ocean, and when he found that I was a naval officer, he was inclined to accord me even greater consideration than formerly. It was difficult for him to believe my assertion that there were but few blacks in my country, and that these occupied a lower social plane than the whites.

Just the reverse is true in Colonel Belik's land. He considered whites inferior beings, creatures of a lower order, and assuring me that even the few white freemen of Abyssinia were never accorded anything approximating a position of social equality with the blacks. They live in the poorer districts of the cities, in little white colonies, and a black who marries a white is socially ostracized.

The arms and ammunition of the Abyssinians are greatly inferior to ours, yet they are tremendously effective against the ill-armed barbarians of Europe. Their rifles are of a type similar to the magazine rifles of twentieth century Pan-America, but carrying only five cartridges in the magazine, in addition to the one in the chamber. They are of extraordinary length, even those of the cavalry; are scientifically rifled, and of extreme accuracy.

The Abyssinians themselves are a fine looking race of black men— tall, muscular, with fine teeth, and regular features, which incline distinctly toward Semitic mold—I refer to the full-blooded natives of Abyssinia. They are the patricians—the aristocracy. The army is officered almost exclusively by them. Among the soldiery a lower type of negro predominates, with thicker lips and broader, flatter noses. These men are recruited, so the colonel told me, from among the conquered tribes of Africa. They are good soldiers—brave and loyal. They can read and write, and they are endowed with a self-confidence and pride which, from my readings of the words of ancient African explorers, must have been wanting in their earliest progenitors. On the whole, it is apparent that the black race has thrived far better in the past two centuries under men of its own color than it had under the domination of whites during all previous history.

I had been a prisoner at the little frontier post for over a month, when orders came to Colonel Belik to hasten to the eastern frontier with the major portion of his command, leaving only one troop to garrison the fort. As his body servant, I accompanied him mounted upon a fiery little Abyssinian pony.

We marched rapidly for ten days through the heart of the ancient German empire, halting when night found us in proximity to water. Often we passed small posts similar to that at which the colonel's regiment had been quartered, finding in each instance that only a single company or troop remained for defence, the balance having been withdrawn toward the northeast, in the same direction in which we were moving.

Naturally, the colonel had not confided to me the nature of his orders; but the rapidity of our march and the fact that all available troops were being hastened toward the northeast assured me that a matter of vital importance to the dominion of Menelek XIV in that part of Europe was threatening or had already broken.

I could not believe that a simple rising of the savage tribes of whites would necessitate the mobilizing of such a force as we presently met with converging from the south into our trail. There were large bodies of cavalry and infantry, endless streams of artillery wagons and guns, and countless horse-drawn covered vehicles laden with camp equipage, munitions, and provisions.

Here, for the first time, I saw camels, great caravans of them, bearing all sorts of heavy burdens, and miles upon miles of elephants doing similar service. It was a scene of wondrous and barbaric splendor, for the men and beasts from the south were gaily caparisoned in rich colors, in marked contrast to the gray uniformed forces of the frontier, with which I had been familiar.

The rumor reached us that Menelek himself was coming, and the pitch of excitement to which this announcement raised the troops was little short of miraculous—at least, to one of my race and nationality whose rulers for centuries had been but ordinary men, holding office at the will of the people for a few brief years.

As I witnessed it, I could not but speculate upon the moral effect upon his troops of a sovereign's presence in the midst of battle. All else being equal in war between the troops of a republic and an empire, could not this exhilarated mental state, amounting almost to hysteria on the part of the imperial troops, weigh heavily against the soldiers of a president? I wonder.

But if the emperor chanced to be absent! What then? Again I wonder.

On the eleventh day we reached our destination—a walled frontier city of about twenty thousand. We passed some lakes, and crossed some old canals before entering the gates. Within, beside the frame buildings, were many built of ancient brick and well-cut stone. These, I was told, were of material taken from the ruins of the ancient city which, once, had stood upon the site of the present town.

The name of the town, translated from the Abyssinian, is New Gondar. It stands, I am convinced, upon the ruins of ancient Berlin, the one time capitol of the old German empire; but except for the old building material used in the new town there is no sign of the former city.

The day after we arrived, the town was gaily decorated with flags, streamers, gorgeous rugs, and banners, for the rumor had proved true— the emperor was coming.

Colonel Belik had accorded me the greatest liberty, permitting me to go where I pleased, after my few duties had been performed. As a result of his kindness, I spent much time wandering about New Gondar, talking with the inhabitants, and exploring this city of black men.

As I had been given a semi-military uniform which bore insignia indicating that I was an officer's body servant, even the blacks treated me with a species of respect, though I could see by their manner that I was really as the dirt beneath their feet. They answered my questions civilly enough; but they would not enter into conversation with me. It was from her slaves that I learned the gossip of the city.

Troops were pouring in from the west and south, and pouring out toward the east. I asked an old slave who was sweeping the dirt into little piles in the gutters of the street where the soldiers were going. He looked at me in surprise.

"Why, to fight the yellow men, of course," he said. "They have crossed the border, and are marching toward New Gondar."

"Who will win?" I asked.

He shrugged his shoulders. "Who knows?" he said. "I hope it will be the yellow men; but Menelek is powerful—it will take many yellow men to defeat him."

Crowds were gathering along the sidewalks to view the emperor's entry into the city. I took my place among them, although I hate crowds, and I am glad that I did, for I witnessed such a spectacle of barbaric splendor as no other Pan-American has ever looked upon.

Down the broad main thoroughfare, which may once have been the historic Unter den Linden, came a brilliant cortege. At the head rode a regiment of red-coated hussars—enormous men, black as night. There were troops of riflemen mounted on camels. The emperor rode in a golden howdah upon the back of a huge elephant so covered with rich hangings and embellished with scintillating gems that scarce more than the beast's eyes and feet were visible.

Menelek was a rather gross looking man, well past middle age, but he carried himself with an air of dignity befitting one descended in unbroken line from the Prophet—as is his claim.

His eyes were bright but crafty, and his features denoted both sensuality and cruelness. In his youth he may have been a rather fine looking black, but when I saw him his appearance was revolting—to me, at least.

Following the emperor came regiment after regiment from the various branches of the service, among them batteries of field guns mounted on elephants.

In the center of the troops following the imperial elephant marched a great caravan of slaves. The old street sweeper at my elbow told me that these were the gifts brought in from the far outlying districts by the commanding officers of the frontier posts. The majority of them were women, destined, I was told, for the harems of the emperor and his favorites. It made my old companion clench his fists to see those poor white women marching past to their horrid fates, and, though I shared his sentiments, I was as powerless to alter their destinies as he.

For a week the troops kept pouring in and out of New Gondar— in always from the south and west; but always toward the east. Each new contingent brought its gifts to the emperor. From the south they brought rugs and ornaments and jewels; from the west, slaves; for the commanding officers of the western frontier posts had naught else to bring.

From the number of women they brought, I judged that they knew the weakness of their imperial master.

And then soldiers commenced coming in from the east, but not with the gay assurance of those who came from the south and west— no, these others came in covered wagons, blood-soaked and suffering. They came at first in little parties of eight or ten, and then they came in fifties, in hundreds, and one day a thousand maimed and dying men were carted into New Gondar.

It was then that Menelek XIV became uneasy. For fifty years his armies had conquered wherever they had marched. At first he had led them in person, lately his presence within a hundred miles of the battle line had been sufficient for large engagements—for minor ones only the knowledge that they were fighting for the glory of their sovereign was necessary to win victories.

One morning, New Gondar was awakened by the booming of cannon. It was the first intimation that the townspeople had received that the enemy was forcing the imperial troops back upon the city. Dust covered couriers galloped in from the front. Fresh troops hastened from the city, and about noon Menelek rode out surrounded by his staff.

For three days thereafter we could hear the cannonading and the spitting of the small arms, for the battle line was scarce two leagues from New Gondar. The city was filled with wounded. Just outside, soldiers were engaged in throwing up earthworks. It was evident to the least enlightened that Menelek expected further reverses.

And then the imperial troops fell back upon these new defenses; or, rather, they were forced back on the enemy. Shells commenced to fall within the city. Menelek returned and took up his headquarters in the stone building that was called the palace. That night came a lull in the hostilities—a truce had been arranged.

Colonel Belik summoned me about seven o'clock to dress him for a function at the palace. In the midst of death and defeat the emperor was about to give a great banquet to his officers. I was to accompany my master and wait upon him—I, Jefferson Turck, lieutenant in the Pan-American navy!

In the privacy of the colonel's quarters I had become accustomed to my menial duties, lightened as they were by the natural kindliness of my master; but the thought of appearing in public as a common slave revolted every fine instinct within me. Yet there was nothing for it but to obey.

I cannot, even now, bring myself to a narration of the humiliation which I experienced that night as I stood behind my black master in silent servility, now pouring his wine, now cutting up his meats for him, now fanning him with a large, plumed fan of feathers.

As fond as I had grown of him, I could have thrust a knife into him, so keenly did I feel the affront that had been put upon me. But at last the long banquet was concluded. The tables were removed. The emperor ascended a dais at one end of the room and seated himself upon a throne, and the entertainment commenced. It was only what ancient history might have led me to expect—musicians, dancing girls, jugglers, and the like.

Near midnight, the master of ceremonies announced that the slave women who had been presented to the emperor since his arrival in New Gondar would be exhibited, that the royal host would select such as he wished, after which he would present the balance of them to his guests. Ah, what royal generosity!

A small door at one side of the room opened, and the poor creatures filed in and were arranged in a long line before the throne. Their backs were toward me. I saw only an occasional profile as now and then a bolder spirit among them turned to survey the apartment and the gorgeous assemblage of officers in their brilliant dress uniforms. They were profiles of young girls, and pretty; but horror was indelibly stamped upon them all. I shuddered as I contemplated their sad fate, and turned my eyes away.

I heard the master of ceremonies command them to prostrate themselves before the emperor, and the sounds as they went upon their knees before him, touching their foreheads to the floor. Then came the official's voice again, in sharp and peremptory command.

"Down, slave!" he cried. "Make obeisance to your sovereign!"

I looked up, attracted by the tone of the man's voice, to see a single, straight, slim figure standing erect in the center of the line of prostrate girls, her arms folded across her breast and little chin in the air. Her back was toward me—I could not see her face, though I should like to see the countenance of this savage young lioness, standing there defiant among that herd of terrified sheep.

"Down! Down!" shouted the master of ceremonies, taking a step toward her and half drawing his sword.

My blood boiled. To stand there, inactive, while a negro struck down that brave girl of my own race! Instinctively I took a forward step to place myself in the man's path; but at the same instant Menelek raised his hand in a gesture that halted the officer. The emperor seemed interested, but in no way angered at the girl's attitude.

"Let us inquire," he said in a smooth, pleasant voice, "why this young woman refuses to do homage to her sovereign," and he put the question himself directly to her.

She answered him in Abyssinian, but brokenly and with an accent that betrayed how recently she had acquired her slight knowledge of the tongue.

"I go on my knees to no one," she said. "I have no sovereign. I myself am sovereign in my own country."

Menelek, at her words, leaned back in his throne and laughed uproariously. Following his example, which seemed always the correct procedure, the assembled guests vied with one another in an effort to laugh more noisily than the emperor.

The girl but tilted her chin a bit higher in the air—even her back proclaimed her utter contempt for her captors. Finally Menelek restored quiet by the simple expedient of a frown, whereupon each loyal guest exchanged his mirthful mien for an emulative scowl.

"And who," asked Menelek, "are you, and by what name is your country called?"

"I am Victory, Queen of Grabritin," replied the girl so quickly and so unexpectedly that I gasped in astonishment.

Chapter IX

Victory! She was here, a slave to these black conquerors. Once more I started toward her; but better judgment held me back—I could do nothing to help her other than by stealth. Could I even accomplish aught by this means? I did not know. It seemed beyond the pale of possibility, and yet I should try.

"And you will not bend the knee to me?" continued Menelek, after she had spoken. Victory shook her head in a most decided negation.

"You shall be my first choice, then," said the emperor. "I like your spirit, for the breaking of it will add to my pleasure in you, and never fear but that it shall be broken—this very night. Take her to my apartments," and he motioned to an officer at his side.

I was surprised to see Victory follow the man off in apparent quiet submission. I tried to follow, that I might be near her against some opportunity to speak with her or assist in her escape; but, after I had followed them from the throne room, through several other apartments, and down a long corridor, I found my further progress barred by a soldier who stood guard before a doorway through which the officer conducted Victory.

Almost immediately the officer reappeared and started back in the direction of the throne room. I had been hiding in a doorway after the guard had turned me back, having taken refuge there while his back was turned, and, as the officer approached me, I withdrew into the room beyond, which was in darkness. There I remained for a long time, watching the sentry before the door of the room in which Victory was a prisoner, and awaiting some favorable circumstance which would give me entry to her.

I have not attempted to fully describe my sensations at the moment I recognized Victory, because, I can assure you, they were entirely indescribable. I should never have imagined that the sight of any human being could affect me as had this unexpected discovery of Victory in the same room in which I was, while I had thought of her for weeks either as dead, or at best hundreds of miles to the west, and as irretrievably lost to me as though she were, in truth, dead.

I was filled with a strange, mad impulse to be near her. It was not enough merely to assist her, or protect her—I desired to touch her—to take her in my arms. I was astounded at myself. Another thing puzzled me—it was my incomprehensible feeling of elation since I had again seen her. With a fate worse than death staring her in the face, and with the knowledge that I should probably die defending her within the hour, I was still happier than I had been for weeks—and all because I had seen again for a few brief minutes the figure of a little heathen maiden. I couldn't account for it, and it angered me; I had never before felt any such sensations in the presence of a woman, and I had made love to some very beautiful ones in my time.

It seemed ages that I stood in the shadow of that doorway, in the ill-lit corridor of the palace of Menelek XIV. A sickly gas jet cast a sad pallor upon the black face of the sentry. The fellow seemed rooted to the spot. Evidently he would never leave, or turn his back again.

I had been in hiding but a short time when I heard the sound of distant cannon. The truce had ended, and the battle had been resumed. Very shortly thereafter the earth shook to the explosion of a shell within the city, and from time to time thereafter other shells burst at no great distance from the palace. The yellow men were bombarding New Gondar again.

Presently officers and slaves commenced to traverse the corridor on matters pertaining to their duties, and then came the emperor, scowling and wrathful. He was followed by a few personal attendants, whom he dismissed at the doorway to his apartments—the same doorway through which Victory had been taken. I chafed to follow him; but the corridor was filled with people. At last they betook themselves to their own apartments, which lay upon either side of the corridor.

An officer and a slave entered the very room in which I hid, forcing me to flatten myself to one side in the darkness until they had passed. Then the slave made a light, and I knew that I must find another hiding place.

Stepping boldly into the corridor, I saw that it was now empty save for the single sentry before the emperor's door. He glanced up as I emerged from the room, the occupants of which had not seen me. I walked straight toward the soldier, my mind made up in an instant. I tried to simulate an expression of cringing servility, and I must have succeeded, for I entirely threw the man off his guard, so that he permitted me to approach within reach of his rifle before stopping me. Then it was too late—for him.

Without a word or a warning, I snatched the piece from his grasp, and, at the same time, struck him a terrific blow between the eyes with my clenched fist. He staggered back in surprise, too dumbfounded even to cry out, and then I clubbed his rifle and felled him with a single mighty blow.

A moment later, I had burst into the room beyond. It was empty!

I gazed about, mad with disappointment. Two doors opened from this to other rooms. I ran to the nearer and listened. Yes, voices were coming from beyond and one was a woman's, level and cold and filled with scorn. There was no terror in it. It was Victory's.

I turned the knob and pushed the door inward just in time to see Menelek seize the girl and drag her toward the far end of the apartment. At the same instant there was a deafening roar just outside the palace—a shell had struck much nearer than any of its predecessors. The noise of it drowned my rapid rush across the room.

But in her struggles, Victory turned Menelek about so that he saw me. She was striking him in the face with her clenched fist, and now he was choking her.

At sight of me, he gave voice to a roar of anger.

"What means this, slave?" he cried. "Out of here! Out of here! Quick, before I kill you!"

But for answer I rushed upon him, striking him with the butt of the rifle. He staggered back, dropping Victory to the floor, and then he cried aloud for the guard, and came at me. Again and again I struck him; but his thick skull might have been armor plate, for all the damage I did it.

He tried to close with me, seizing the rifle, but I was stronger than he, and, wrenching the weapon from his grasp, tossed it aside and made for his throat with my bare hands. I had not dared fire the weapon for fear that its report would bring the larger guard stationed at the farther end of the corridor.

We struggled about the room, striking one another, knocking over furniture, and rolling upon the floor. Menelek was a powerful man, and he was fighting for his life. Continually he kept calling for the guard, until I succeeded in getting a grip upon his throat; but it was too late. His cries had been heard, and suddenly the door burst open, and a score of armed guardsmen rushed into the apartment.

Victory seized the rifle from the floor and leaped between me and them. I had the black emperor upon his back, and both my hands were at his throat, choking the life from him.

The rest happened in the fraction of a second. There was a rending crash above us, then a deafening explosion within the chamber. Smoke and powder fumes filled the room. Half stunned, I rose from the lifeless body of my antagonist just in time to see Victory stagger to her feet and turn toward me. Slowly the smoke cleared to reveal the shattered remnants of the guard. A shell had fallen through the palace roof and exploded just in the rear of the detachment of guardsmen who were coming to the rescue of their emperor. Why neither Victory nor I were struck is a miracle. The room was a wreck. A great, jagged hole was torn in the ceiling, and the wall toward the corridor had been blown entirely out.

As I rose, Victory had risen, too, and started toward me; but when she saw that I was uninjured she stopped, and stood there in the center of the demolished apartment looking at me. Her expression was inscrutable— I could not guess whether she was glad to see me, or not.

"Victory!" I cried. "Thank God that you are safe!" And I approached her, a greater gladness in my heart than I had felt since the moment that I knew the *Coldwater* must be swept beyond 30.

There was no answering gladness in her eyes. Instead, she stamped her little foot in anger.

"Why did it have to be you who saved me!" she exclaimed. "I hate you!"

"Hate me?" I asked. "Why should you hate me, Victory? I do not hate you. I—I—." What was I about to say? I was very close to her as a great light broke over me. Why had I never realized it before? The truth accounted for a great many hitherto inexplicable moods that had claimed me from time to time since first I had seen Victory.

"Why should I hate you?" she repeated. "Because Snider told me— he told me that you had promised me to him; but he did not get me. I killed him, as I should like to kill you!"

"Snider lied!" I cried; and then I seized her and held her in my arms, and made her listen to me, though she struggled and fought like a young lioness. "I love you, Victory. You must know that I love you—that I have always loved you, and that I never could have made so base a promise."

She ceased her struggles, just a trifle; but still tried to push me from her. "You called me a barbarian!" she said.

Ah, so that was it! That still rankled. I crushed her to me.

"You could not love a barbarian," she went on; but she had ceased to struggle.

"But I do love a barbarian, Victory!" I cried; "the dearest barbarian in the world."

She raised her eyes to mine, and then her smooth, brown arms encircled my neck and drew my lips down to hers.

"I love you—I have loved you always!" she said, and then she buried her face upon my shoulder and sobbed. "I have been so unhappy," she said; "but I could not die while I thought that you might live."

As we stood there, momentarily forgetful of all else than our new found happiness, the ferocity of the bombardment increased until scarce thirty seconds elapsed between the shells that rained about the palace.

To remain long would be to invite certain death. We could not escape the way that we had entered the apartment, for not only was the corridor now choked with debris, but beyond the corridor there were doubtless many members of the emperor's household who would stop us.

Upon the opposite side of the room was another door, and toward this I led the way. It opened into a third apartment with windows overlooking an inner court. From one of these windows I surveyed the courtyard. Apparently it was empty, and the rooms upon the opposite side were unlighted.

Assisting Victory to the open, I followed, and together we crossed the court, discovering upon the opposite side a number of wide, wooden doors set in the wall of the palace, with small windows between. As we stood close behind one of the doors, listening, a horse within neighed.

"The stables!" I whispered; and, a moment later, had pushed back a door and entered. From the city about us we could hear the din of great commotion, and quite close the sounds of battle—the crack of thousands of rifles, the yells of the soldiers, the hoarse commands of officers, and the blare of bugles.

The bombardment had ceased as suddenly as it had commenced. I judged that the enemy was storming the city, for the sounds we heard were the sounds of hand-to-hand combat.

Within the stables I groped about until I had found saddles and bridles for two horses; but afterward, in the darkness, I could find but a single mount. The doors of the opposite side, leading to the street, were open, and we could see great multitudes of men, women, and children fleeing toward the west. Soldiers, afoot and mounted, were joining the mad exodus. Now and then a camel or an elephant would pass bearing some officer or dignitary to safety. It was evident that the city would fall at any moment—a fact which was amply proclaimed by the terror-stricken haste of the fear-mad mob.

Horse, camel, and elephant trod helpless women and children beneath their feet. A common soldier dragged a general from his mount, and, leaping to the animal's back, fled down the packed street toward the west. A woman seized a gun and brained a court dignitary, whose horse had trampled her child to death. Shrieks, curses, commands, supplications filled the air. It was a frightful scene—one that will be burned upon my memory forever.

I had saddled and bridled the single horse which had evidently been overlooked by the royal household in its flight, and, standing a little back in the shadow of the stable's interior, Victory and I watched the surging throng without.

To have entered it would have been to have courted greater danger than we were already in. We decided to wait until the stress of blacks thinned, and for more than an hour we stood there while the sounds of battle raged upon the eastern side of the city and the population flew toward the west. More and more numerous became the uniformed soldiers among the fleeing throng, until, toward the last, the street was packed with them. It was no orderly retreat; but a rout, complete and terrible.

The fighting was steadily approaching us now, until the crack of rifles sounded in the very street upon which we were looking. And then came a handful of brave men—a little rear guard backing slowly toward the west, working their smoking rifles in feverish haste as they fired volley after volley at the foe we could not see.

But these were pressed back and back until the first line of the enemy came opposite our shelter. They were men of medium height, with olive complexions and almond eyes. In them I recognized the descendants of the ancient Chinese race.

They were well uniformed and superbly armed, and they fought bravely and under perfect discipline. So rapt was I in the exciting events transpiring in the street that I did not hear the approach of a body of men from behind. It was a party of the conquerors who had entered the palace and were searching it.

They came upon us so unexpectedly that we were prisoners before we realized what had happened. That night we were held under a strong guard just outside the eastern wall of the city, and the next morning were started upon a long march toward the east.

Our captors were not unkind to us, and treated the women prisoners with respect. We marched for many days—so many that I lost count of them—and at last we came to another city—a Chinese city this time—which stands upon the site of ancient Moscow.

It is only a small frontier city; but it is well built and well kept. Here a large military force is maintained, and here also, is a terminus of the railroad that crosses modern China to the Pacific.

There was every evidence of a high civilization in all that we saw within the city, which, in connection with the humane treatment that had been accorded all prisoners upon the long and tiresome march, encouraged me to hope that I might appeal to some high office here for the treatment which my rank and birth merited.

We could converse with our captors only through the medium of interpreters who spoke both Chinese and Abyssinian; but there were many of these, and shortly after we reached the city I persuaded one of them to carry a verbal message to the officer who had commanded the troops during the return from New Gondar, asking that I might be given a hearing by some high official.

The reply to my request was a summons to appear before the officer to whom I had addressed my appeal. A sergeant came for me along with the interpreter, and I managed to obtain his permission to let Victory accompany me—I had never left her alone with the prisoners since we had been captured.

To my delight I found that the officer into whose presence we were conducted spoke Abyssinian fluently. He was astounded when I told him that I was a Pan-American. Unlike all others whom I had spoken with since my arrival in Europe, he was well acquainted with ancient history—was familiar with twentieth century conditions in Pan-America, and after putting a half dozen questions to me was satisfied that I spoke the truth.

When I told him that Victory was Queen of England he showed little surprise, telling me that in their recent explorations in ancient Russia they had found many descendants of the old nobility and royalty.

He immediately set aside a comfortable house for us, furnished us with servants and with money, and in other ways showed us every attention and kindness.

He told me that he would telegraph his emperor at once, and the result was that we were presently commanded to repair to Peking and present ourselves before the ruler.

We made the journey in a comfortable railway carriage, through a country which, as we traveled farther toward the east, showed increasing evidence of prosperity and wealth.

At the imperial court we were received with great kindness, the emperor being most inquisitive about the state of modern Pan-America. He told me that while he personally deplored the existence of the strict regulations which had raised a barrier between the east and the west, he had felt, as had his predecessors, that recognition of the wishes of the great Pan-American federation would be most conductive to the continued peace of the world.

His empire includes all of Asia, and the islands of the Pacific as far east as 175W. The empire of Japan no longer exists, having been conquered and absorbed by China over a hundred year ago. The Philippines are well administered, and constitute one of the most progressive colonies of the Chinese empire.

The emperor told me that the building of this great empire and the spreading of enlightenment among its diversified and savage peoples had required all the best efforts of nearly two hundred years. Upon his accession to the throne he had found the labor well nigh perfected and had turned his attention to the reclamation of Europe.

His ambition is to wrest it from the hands of the blacks, and then to attempt the work of elevating its fallen peoples to the high estate from which the Great War precipitated them.

I asked him who was victorious in that war; and he shook his head sadly as he replied:

"Pan-America, perhaps, and China, with the blacks of Abyssinia," he said. "Those who did not fight were the only ones to reap any of the rewards that are supposed to belong to victory. The combatants repeated naught but annihilation. You have seen—better than any man you must realize that there was no victory for any nation embroiled in that frightful war."

"When did it end?" I asked him.

Again he shook his head. "It has not ended yet. There has never been a formal peace declared in Europe—after a while there were none left to make peace, and the rude tribes which sprang from the survivors continued to fight among themselves because they knew no better condition of society. War razed the works of men—war and pestilence razed man. God give that there shall never be such another war!"

You all know how Porfirio Johnson returned to Pan-America with John Alvarez in chains; how Alvarez's trial raised a popular demonstration that the government could not ignore. His eloquent appeal—not for himself, but for me—is historic, as are its results. You know how a fleet was sent across the Atlantic to search for me, how the restrictions against crossing 30 to 175 were removed forever, and how the officers were brought to Peking, arriving upon the very day that Victory and I were married at the imperial court.

My return to Pan-America was very different from anything I could possibly have imagined a year before. Instead of being received as a traitor to my country, I was acclaimed a hero. It was good to get back again, good to witness the kindly treatment that was accorded my dear Victory, and when I learned that Delcarte and Taylor had been found at the mouth of the Rhine and were already back in Pan-America my joy was unalloyed.

And now we are going back, Victory and I, with the men and the munitions and power to reclaim England for her queen. Again I shall cross 30; but under what altered conditions!

A new epoch for Europe is inaugurated, with enlightened China on the east and enlightened Pan-America on the west—the two great peace powers whom God has preserved to regenerate chastened and forgiven Europe. I have been through much—I have suffered much; but I have won two great laurel wreaths beyond 30. One is the opportunity to rescue Europe from barbarism, the other is a little barbarian, and the greater of these is—Victory.

PHILLIP R. BURGER

The War to End All Future Wars

Tarzan had made Edgar Rice Burroughs the golden boy of the pulp magazine circuit; nevertheless the author still managed to collect a few rejection slips. In bouncing his 1915 novel *Beyond Thirty*, Bob Davis of *All-Story Magazine* assessed the work as "a magnificent piece of scenery with no play." His critique continued, "You have drawn an extraordinary picture and set the stage for a stupendous thing. Then the curtain falls."[1] Burroughs meticulously creates an intriguing future history—but doesn't do much with it. The protagonist Jefferson Turck of the Pan-American Federation meets degenerate Europeans, the powerful Abyssinian army, and the benevolent Chinese, yet he never really participates in the action; he mostly observes. He even manages to remain fully clothed throughout the tale, while most of Burroughs's heroes get stripped naked pretty early on.

Beyond Thirty presents a vision of what the world might have been like two centuries into the future had the United States continued to maintain its policy of isolation from the conflict then raging in Europe. Well, President Woodrow Wilson would formally declare war upon the Central Powers on 6 April 1917, undermining the foundation of Burroughs's entire scenario. The story appeared only once in Burroughs's lifetime, in the February 1916 issue of the obscure *All-Around Magazine*. Even Burroughs must have thought it dated, as he never issued the tale in book form from his own publishing house.[2]

Science fiction has the reputation of being a genre of prediction, and the accuracy of the prediction is often the basis for how such literature is judged. But prediction was not on Burroughs's mind when he wrote his tale. *Beyond Thirty* has little to do with the year 2137 and everything to do with the year 1915. In his classic study *Voices Prophesying War*, I. F. Clarke noted that "the outbreak of the First World War caused some Americans to turn to fiction as a means of warning their countrymen against the dangers of remaining unprepared in a warring world."[3] Burroughs, ultra-patriot that he was, followed this trend in *Beyond Thirty*. Though his gloomy descriptions of a bombed-out Europe give his novel the patina of an antiwar tract, Burroughs's intent was exactly the opposite. By exaggerating both the effects of the European conflict and America's response, Burroughs was advising his country to see to its own military preparedness and possible involvement in the Great War. In issuing this call Burroughs also revealed much about how he and many Americans felt toward Europe, politics, race, and the "fighting spirit" of modern nations.

Burroughs wrote *Beyond Thirty* while the United States stood back and watched as "blood-frenzied Europe" tore its own house apart. For most Americans the war at first was distant and unimportant. But repeated U-boat predations on neutral shipping, particularly the torpedoing of the *Lusitania* on 7 May 1915, brought an upswell of anti-German sentiment. President Wilson's public response to the *Lusitania* incident was a declaration that America remained "too proud to fight." Burroughs's creative response was to take the Wilson policy of isolationism to its absurd limit, making the policy a "fetish which has ruled Pan-Americans for two centuries, and which is based upon a blind faith in the infallibility of the prescience of the long-dead framers of the articles of the Pan-American federation." For Burroughs, a policy initiated in response to something viewed as a *European* matter was in time a policy to be lampooned.

While Europe bled, the debate raged in America between the pacifists, who felt that a military buildup increased the possibility of war, and the militarists, who adhered to the policy, in the Reagan parlance, of peace through strength. Neither side could make sense of the other. "As we have outgrown the duel, so have we outgrown homicidal war," Andrew Carnegie assessed in 1913, his statement striking us as so optimistic that even Pollyanna would blush. While there were no war clouds on America's horizon, Carnegie proceeded from the assumption that his country was separate from the rest of the world, leading him to profess a rather myopic view of world relations: "Has there ever been danger of war between Germany and ourselves, members of the same Teutonic race? Never has it been imagined."[4] Alas, even the hoary notion of "race loyalty" couldn't survive the upcoming madness that would envelop the world. Two years later, with the European war in full swing, Theodore Roosevelt assessed such a philosophy succinctly: "The one certain way to invite disaster is to be opulent, offensive, and unarmed."[5] Roosevelt apparently believed that America was all three.

Roosevelt was Burroughs's political hero, and now out of the highest office he was using a pen rather than a big stick to affect American opinion. Neutrality bred passivity, which would lead to a weakened nation. Only military training could halt this inevitable slide. "All the youth of the nation should be trained in warlike exercises," advised Roosevelt, "and in the use of arms—as well as in the indispensable virtues of courage, self restraint, and endurance—so as to be fit for natural defense."[6] Burroughs echoes Roosevelt's stand when his character Jefferson Turck expresses the opinion that "military training was necessary for the salvation of personal courage in the Pan-American race." The Pan-American alliance of *Beyond Thirty* has enjoyed two centuries of "peace, prosperity and happiness," not because it failed to join the European war, but because it prepared itself, both physically and mentally, for the time when war would come. Such a state of preparedness was what Burroughs wished for his country at the time he wrote *Beyond Thirty*.

Militarily speaking, the United States was not entirely up to snuff at the outbreak of World War I. Its standing army was negligible, leading Burroughs to remark in a 1914 article that America had "an army that half a dozen of the new Krupp guns would wipe out of existence in about forty-seven minutes."[7] The U.S. navy was third in the world, behind England and Germany, and had been built up most vigorously during Roosevelt's presidential watch. Still, there was a fair amount of modernizing left to do, as Burroughs hints at in *Beyond Thirty*. For example, the aerosub Jefferson Turck finds himself in command of is a decrepit old bucket, "but the world-old parsimony of government retained her in active service." Although President Wilson would continue with Roosevelt's naval modernization plans, Burroughs's presentation of the future navy reveals his opinion that Wilson's overall approach was rather timid. The Pan-American navy, "the greatest argument for peace the world had ever known," was little more than a glorified version of the Coast Guard—an organization that had been cobbled together from several existing agencies in early 1915.

With the Civil War now a generation in the past, and with recent splendid little wars in Cuba and the Philippines, many Americans viewed war as a romantic—and quickly concluded—escapade. So did Burroughs. His father had served in the Civil War, and his own military itch still needed to be scratched. His youthful stint in the frontier cavalry had been a disappointment; Roosevelt had not wanted him for the Rough Riders; and he would be too old when the United States declared war on Germany to "go over the top and spear a Hun," as he evidently wanted to do.[8] Burroughs's fiction reflects this naive view of war. His early Mars and Pellucidar tales detail wars that consist of lightning-like raids and decisive victories. In "Barney Custer of Beatrice" (the second half of the book *The Mad King* and written in late 1914) the mythical Balkan kingdom of Lutha joins forces with Serbia to repel an Austrian invasion, with Barney Custer of Nebraska in the disguise of King Leopold leading the charge. Two days of fighting ensure a lasting peace. Sequels were not forthcoming; the real world was casting a shadow over his Ruritanian fantasy.

Unlike the United States, Europe had lost all sense of war as a romantic escapade; new technologies had turned it into an all-consuming destructive force. But from an American standpoint the unending stalemate of the Great War was indicative of how Europe as a whole had lost the "fighting spirit." Many of Burroughs's books express the idea that European society and culture had grown soft, in need of a little American virility (we're a young country after all). In *The Mad King* only Nebraskan Barney Custer is worthy of sitting on the throne of tiny Lutha. In *The Land That Time Forgot* Bowen Tyler of California takes command of a boatload of British and German sailors. In the

Pellucidar novels David Innes of Connecticut goes Europe one better and creates an empire without colonial oppression. In *Beyond Thirty* Jefferson Turck declares: "I am glad that [the chance] was given to me to be an instrument in the hands of Providence for the uplifting of benighted Europe, and the amelioration of the suffering, degradation, and abysmal ignorance in which I found her." Europe can be led out of her intellectually and morally backward condition (to use one definition of "benighted") only by the United States. Burroughs wanted his country to take war to the Kaiser and thus save Europe from itself.

Burroughs, like all Americans, became acquainted (in a somewhat watered-down fashion) through newspapers and magazines with how wars were now being fought. Civilized rules of warfare no longer applied—the *Lusitania* incident had shown that—and so in *Beyond Thirty* Burroughs literalizes the American opinion that Europeans were fighting a barbaric war by having their war turn them into barbarians. When Americans finally joined the fray their justification for fighting was to stem German aggression and to make the world safe for democracy. Europe's reasons for starting the war in the first place were more convoluted, if not downright mystifying to Americans: Europe seemed to be fighting merely for the sake of fighting. America's reasons for fighting were noble; Europe's reasons for fighting were petty. The war of *Beyond Thirty* had no end because it was fought for no high ideal.

With the arrival of the Abyssinian and Chinese forces upon his future world stage, Burroughs creatively engages in the common American practice of criticizing Europe's colonial activities. Sure, the United States had recently acquired some extensive overseas territories, but we were setting up camp in the Philippines, the Dominican Republic and elsewhere only "to help" our "little brown brothers" in achieving their goal of self-rule. Europe's overseas activities were simply a matter of exploitation. One of Burroughs's favorite literary techniques was to flip-flop the perceived racial pecking order (*Gods of Mars* being the most elaborate example). In *Beyond Thirty* this technique results in the ironic scenario of the great European powers being colonized by their former colonies. Unfortunately this is also the most underdeveloped section of the novel, and in playing upon two of white America's many xenophobic worries—that of the "Negro problem" and the "yellow peril"—Burroughs sends conflicting signals as to what his own racial attitudes may have been.

Burroughs's personal history includes some intriguing multiethnic encounters. He had spent a brief period in the 1890s with the Seventh U.S. Cavalry in Arizona. Sharing quarters at Fort Grant was the Twenty-fourth Infantry, one of the famed black regiments of American frontier history, and Burroughs often found himself assigned to work details under the watchful eyes of black superiors. They were "wonderful soldiers and as hard as nails," Burroughs recalled in his unpublished autobiography, and "without exception they were excellent men who took no advantage of their authority over us and on the whole were better to work under than our own white sergeants."[9] The images of these soldiers gave Burroughs some of the necessary grist for his creative mill when describing the conquests of the Abyssinian emperor Menelik XIV in *Beyond Thirty*—that, and recent history. Menelik II had died in 1913; twenty years earlier he had made a distinct impression upon the Western world when his forces defeated an invading Italian army. The sole African kingdom to have avoided a colonial fate became in Burroughs's hands a major colonial power.

Yet Burroughs does not make clear whether his presentation of race reversal is an enlightened satire on the racial situation in the United States or a swipe at the notion of black equality. Between 1910 and 1920 Burroughs's home town of Chicago saw a major influx of southern blacks, primarily into the city's south side, which led the white populace to worry about "darkies" taking jobs, decreasing property values, and posing a threat to white womanhood. Now compare this to the future world of *Beyond Thirty*. Free whites of Abyssinia are considered socially and genetically inferior by the black majority and are forced to live in the poorest sections of the cities in "white colonies." Trade black for white and you have a description of how the America of Burroughs's time treated urban blacks. Burroughs *may* have wanted readers to think about his country's treatment of its black citizens, but he muddies the waters when he describes in greater detail the African troops. The numerically small officer class—"tall, muscular, with fine teeth, and regular features"—controls a vast army composed of "a lower type of negro . . . with thicker lips and broader, flatter noses." The irony of this reverse colonial scenario must give way to a contemporary worry: a white "nation" being invaded by brutish blacks.

Burroughs manages to be both progressive in his portrayal of the Abyssinians as an educated, disciplined, and efficient military force and stereotypical when he portrays Africans as lustful brutes. Having it both ways allows Burroughs's readers, in the historian Richard Slotkin's assessment, "the double satisfaction of affiliating with an ethic of tolerance while enjoying the violent expression of racialist antipathies."[10] In other words, a writer can represent blacks in a heroic manner while also utilizing black stereotypes to satisfy the requirements of popular fiction, thus reaffirming the white readership's understanding of the "proper" order of the races. Modern critics, as a result, constantly debate whether or not Burroughs was a racist because it is impossible to determine if he ascribed to one view or the other.

With the introduction of the Chinese empire in the closing pages of *Beyond Thirty* Burroughs brings another xenophobic worry of white America to the fore. Sax Rohmer's brilliant but evil Dr. Fu Manchu, "all the cruel cunning of an entire Eastern race" in one inscrutable package, came to personify for pulp readers the dreaded "yellow peril." This particular racial worry—"this persistent vision of the Chinese race, roused from its long lethargy, and feverishly arming itself for wars of conquest and revenge" as one contemporaneous journalist mockingly labeled it[11]—took hold because a) all Asians supposedly thought alike, and b) there were so many of them. Japan's recent success in its war with Russia forced the West to take notice of a growing power across the Pacific. China in 1915 had fallen into civil conflict after the collapse of the Manchu dynasty and represented a less-than-negligible threat. Yet the worry over the "yellow peril" was still there, and presenting the Chinese as having a martial interest similar to that of the Japanese was an easy step for a pulp writer to take. Just give the Chinese a capable leader (in *Beyond Thirty* Burroughs teases with an early reference to a nameless "military power . . . [that] rose so suddenly in China") and the so-called yellow hordes will march all over Europe.

But Burroughs upsets the early-twentieth-century racial apple cart yet again by making the Chinese the good guys in his racial tableau. He renders very few details to his Chinese empire, which appears so late in the game. Its presence is more of a plot device needed to wrap the story up. Unlike the Abyssinians, who were motivated by colonial conquest, Burroughs's Chinese seek only to spread enlightenment to the dark corners of the world, making their empire building similar to the United States' overseas efforts (at least as perceived by Americans). It is difficult to determine why Burroughs stood the "yellow peril" on its head, although there is one peculiar aspect in his personal history that may have influenced his presentation: back in 1906 Burroughs, still seeking any kind of military glory, pursued a commission in the Chinese army. The Imperial Chinese Legation flatly turned him down, replying: "[T]here are no openings in the Chinese army for American officers or any other nationality."[12] One should be grateful that they did so, but through his fictional persona of Jefferson Turck, however, Burroughs was finally able to serve the Chinese emperor.

Perhaps typical for a militarist repeatedly denied military involvement, Burroughs emerged from the Great War with a hyper form of patriotism that carried some less-than-savory elements, particularly his routing of any anti-American activity at home. "It is very possible that we shall see loosed upon the community a raft of street-corner orators of the IWW and Bolshevik types," he wrote in a high-strung article. "We have thrashed the trouble makers of Europe and it's within the range of possibilities that we may have to deal with similar cattle here."[13] His paranoid patriotism would pop up under the guise of fiction and include occasional digs at labor organizers, pacifists, ethnic minorities, and many others outside the American mainstream. That meant there was quite a herd of cattle out there indeed.

Luckily Burroughs never got beyond the ranting stage, but he would continue to trumpet through his fiction the call for military preparedness that he had begun with *Beyond Thirty*. In *The Moon Maid* (1922) Burroughs presents us with another version of the Great War—this one ending in 1967 with the "absolute domination of the Anglo-Saxon race over all the other races of the world" and a subsequent mass disarmament. Thus the Anglo-Saxon race sets itself up for conquest by invaders from the moon, invaders with all the perceived characteristics of Bolsheviks, the growing urban black population, Eastern European immigrants, "the offspring of generations of menials and servants"—all the worries of white, middle-class America rolled up into one xenophobic package. Obviously Burroughs didn't care for his country's postwar disarmament binge.

Having not experienced war first hand, and feeling embarrassed that he could not participate in the great crusade, Burroughs would pepper stories with the message that war was a Good Thing. In *Tarzan and the Ant Men* (1923) he gives the "good" (American) and "bad" (European) reasons for entering onto the field of battle: "No chicanery of politics here, no thinly veiled ambition of some potential tyrant . . . but patriotism of purest strain energized by the powerful urge of self-preservation." If this message wasn't clear enough, he was even more pointed in *Master Mind of Mars* (1925), where he has one character declare: "War never brought peace—it but brings more and greater wars. . . . Peace should be considered only as a time for preparation for the principal business of man's existence." Cynical perhaps, but it sounds like Burroughs talking. It's time to get out the big stick.

By the time he wrote "Beyond the Farthest Star" (1940) Burroughs seemed to be on the road to a more mature view concerning the horrors of war. In this story Burroughs depicts a planet entering its second century of a war that dwarfs all earthly efforts in that arena. So costly and debilitating is this constant state of military preparedness in both human and material terms that the only solution to the conflict is for one side to evacuate the planet. Burroughs never got around to recording this proposed migration—in fact, the Second World War intervened. Then entering his seventies Burroughs got a gig as a war correspondent in the Pacific, and it became his grand adventure. Even in old age a youthful enthusiasm for war resurfaced. For a man whose stories celebrate perpetual youth—and whose stories are perpetually appealing to youthful readers—such passion is not all that surprising. Burroughs may have recognized the horrors of modern war, but he wouldn't have missed the war for the world.

In 1915 Edgar Rice Burroughs imagined a future of incessant warfare that the United States mercifully avoided. As prediction then, *Beyond Thirty* was only 50 percent accurate. Bob Davis's editorial assessment of the story achieved the same odds. While there may not be much of a play within this "magnificent piece of scenery," there is plenty occurring off stage. One just has to step behind the curtain to see it all.

NOTES

An earlier version of this article appeared under the title "The Uplifting of Benighted Europe" in *Burroughs Bulletin*, n.s., 30 (spring 1997): 26–30.

1. Letter of 7 September 1915, quoted in Irwin Porges, *Edgar Rice Burroughs: The Man Who Created Tarzan* (Provo UT: Brigham Young University Press, 1975), 257. *Beyond Thirty* was written between 8 July and 10 August 1915.

2. Hugo Gernsback, editor of *Amazing Stories*, did express an interest in reprinting the novel, but he and Burroughs could not come to a mutually satisfactory monetary agreement. See Sam Moskowitz, "Hugo Gernsback and Edgar Rice Burroughs," *Burroughs Bulletin*, n.s., 21 (January 1995): 3–9.

3. I. F. Clarke, *Voices Prophesying War: Future Wars 1763–3749*, 2nd ed. (New York: Oxford University Press, 1992), 2.

4. Andrew Carnegie, "The Baseless Fear of War," *The Independent* 74 (13 February 1913): 346.

5. Theodore Roosevelt, *America and the World War* (New York: Charles Scribner's Sons, 1915), 136.

6. Roosevelt, *America and the World War,* 159.

7. Edgar Rice Burroughs, "What Is the Matter with the United States Army?" unpublished article quoted in Porges, *Edgar Rice Burroughs*, 211. The article is not dated but was probably written in mid-1914.

8. Edgar Rice Burroughs, "Home Guarding for the Liberty Loan," Flag Day speech delivered 14 June 1918 in Oak Park IL; quoted in Porges, *Edgar Rice Burroughs*, 288.

9. Quoted in Porges, *Edgar Rice Burroughs,* 60.

10. Richard Slotkin, *Gunfighter Nation: The Myth of the Frontier in Twentieth-Century America* (New York: Harper Collins, 1993), 211.

11. J. O. P. Bland, "The Yellow Peril," *Living Age* 273 (22 June 1912): 708.

12. Letter of 20 March 1906, quoted in Porges, *Edgar Rice Burroughs,* 97.

13. Edgar Rice Burroughs, "Peace and the Militia," 16 November 1918, quoted in Porges, *Edgar Rice Burroughs*, 289. The publication in which the article originally appeared is unknown.

Beyond 1965, Beyond 2137, Beyond 30

It was the early 1960s when I first read *Beyond Thirty*, and yesterday I read it again. For a moment I sat at my desk, comparing my reactions to the story after these two readings, trying to remember just what struck me about *Beyond Thirty* nearly forty years ago, but I am lucky— I had put down my reaction to the story back in the sixties and had incorporated those thoughts into my own, very first, book: *Edgar Rice Burroughs: Master of Adventure* (1965).

In that era I lived in New York and held down two jobs. In one I was a technical writer and editor, turning out user manuals for a huge electronics company. In the other I edited books for a small publisher called Canaveral Press. At the electronics firm I worked in comfortable, modern surroundings with congenial colleagues. My office was in midtown, in the Time & Life Building across Sixth Avenue from Radio City Music Hall. While working there I became acquainted with a few *Life* magazine writers and even picked up an occasional consulting fee (although never a byline) from the magazine. My own paychecks, while not huge, were adequate for the needs of a young professional with a growing family. I was also frustrated and bored to tears.

At Canaveral Press I did work that I loved. The company was owned by Jack Biblo and Jack Tannen, two classic bookmen of the old school. The company shared office space with Biblo and Tannen's bookstore on Fourth Avenue below Fourteenth Street, New York's once legendary Book Row. Biblo and Tannen's was a magical establishment whose architecture might have been designed by M. C. Escher. There I could spend hours wandering through galleries and cul-de-sacs, up and down creaking ancient staircases, exploring attics, basements, and sub-basements that extended down to the level of Manhattan's bedrock. The whole place was filled with well-read and well-loved volumes of poetry and history and biography and philosophy and science and criticism and fiction.

As editor for Canaveral Press I worked with the likes of James Blish, Edward Elmer Smith (the legendary "Doc" Smith of science fiction), L. Sprague de Camp, and Catherine Crook de Camp. I worked with brilliant artists and hard-bitten printers. I bought some manuscripts that I dearly loved and rejected others, some with regret, some (I must confess) with ill-concealed glee.

It was a glorious job; Canaveral Press was my heaven.

My situation there was also, however, a clear-cut case of *Don't Quit Your Day Job*.

The mainstay of our fiction line was the works of Edgar Rice Burroughs, and when a manuscript for an essay about Burroughs outgrew its allotted space, the two Jacks asked me to go ahead and expand it further into a book. Thus was launched my career as an author in my own right, and thus I found myself striving to track down every published work of Edgar Rice Burroughs, which came to nearly seventy books and a number of uncollected short stories. Hulbert Burroughs, who is no longer with us but at that time was running affairs from Tarzana, gave me access to unpublished manuscripts as well. This research led to my first encounter with *Beyond Thirty*.

The short novel had appeared first in *All Around* magazine in 1916. After that it remained out of print until the 1950s when two "gray market" editions were published. These versions were not authorized by the Burroughs estate, but they probably were not illegal either, in view of the tangled condition of the Burroughs copyrights.

While reading the book the first time I had mixed feelings. Neither its protagonist and narrator, Jefferson Turck, nor any of its other characters are among Burroughs's stronger creations. Its plot is also somewhat weak, with an oddity of pacing to add to the novel's difficulty. Its earliest pages are devoted to establishing background—what television writers sometimes call "laying pipe"—during which almost nothing actually happens.

Burroughs then moves on to a tale of shipwreck and adventure in a feral future world. All of this is standard fare for Burroughs, of course, and was in fact common currency in the pages of the pulp magazines for which he wrote. The fights with hairy savages, the battles with tigers and lions, and the discovery of a seminude barbarian queen could all have been lifted from (or dropped into) any of a score of Burroughs's jungle tales, interplanetary escapades, or hollow-world romances—or into the stories of Arthur Conan Doyle, Louis Holberg, Frank R. Stockton, H. Rider Haggard, George Allan England, Jack London, or a hundred other Victorian and Edwardian fabulists industriously at work in Britain, the United States, and other countries.

It is only when Turck is captured by the armies of the Abyssinian Empire that the book turns in a distinctive direction: we are shown an advanced black African civilization from the viewpoint of a white slave. Unfortunately, this portion of the novel is somewhat hurried. When Burroughs introduces still another surprising civilization, that of a future China, he shifts into a still higher gear. The more fascinating the landscape, the faster Burroughs's narrative vehicle races.

Eighty-five years after the fact, one can only wonder why *Beyond Thirty* is so—for want of a better word—misshapen. Was Burroughs under pressure to get the manuscript off his desk, so he could move on to other projects? Did he feel that he had bitten off more than he could chew? Had the story gotten out of control, forcing its author to take desperate means to recapture his own creation? Any of these explanations is possible.

Even in this misshapen book, Burroughs's projected "future history" is a grand, impressive achievement. But also of importance are his revealed attitudes regarding heredity, race, and war. Here is what I consider the key paragraph of my comments on *Beyond Thirty*, as written in 1965:

The remarkable anticipation of Orwell's *1984* in Burroughs's idea of wiping entire portions of history from schoolbooks was noted by Paul Mandel in his excellent article for *Life* magazine on Burroughs, published in November, 1963. The equally remarkable anticipation of the growth of Chinese power "after the fall of the republic," the new Chinese Empire turning first to Manchuria, Korea, and the Philippines, and then westward to Europe, is positively chilling in its accuracy. And the prediction of an African Empire challenging China for supremacy is a matter which may be presaged today in the fledgling Organization of African Unity— with its headquarters in Addis Ababa, the ancient seat of the Meneleks!

In fact there were only two Meneleks (or Meneliks) who ruled in Ethiopia, and only one of them was ancient. It was the second Menelik who was probably—I would say, almost certainly—in Burroughs's mind when he wrote *Beyond Thirty*. Born in 1844, Menelik II began his ascent to power in 1868 and finally occupied the temporarily vacant throne of Ethiopia (ancient Abyssinia) in 1889. He had obtained Italian backing for his seizure of power and quickly concluded a treaty with Italy. When that nation used this agreement (the Treaty of Ucialli) as an excuse for establishing a protectorate in Ethiopia and sent troops to occupy the country, Menelik went to war. His army defeated and humiliated the Italian force at the battle of Aduwa, gaining full recognition of Ethiopia's independence and even forcing Italy to pay an indemnity.

The defeat of a modern European army by a force of African "savages" sent shock waves through Europe. While attenuated by distance, the shock would have reached America in short order. The European experience in Africa had been one of colonial masters ruling subjugated indigenous peoples. The American experience with Africans had been on its own land through the institution of slavery. The American Civil War had taken place just a half-century earlier. Substantial numbers of Confederate veterans and former slaveholders still survived, as did former slaves and their children. Jim Crow laws were common. To white Americans, an image of a black African army triumphing over a white European force was surely a terrifying one, while to black Americans it represented liberation and vengeful justice.

Menelik II lived until 1913, and his demise, specifically, seems likely to have stimulated the thinking that led Burroughs to *Beyond Thirty*.

(Oh, and I did not mention that back in 1965 I had picked up a consulting fee from *Life* for helping Paul Mandel with his "excellent article.")

It is clear from many of Burroughs's works that he believed in a kind of natural aristocracy. One need only compare the innate nobility of Tarzan or the inevitability of John Carter's rise in Barsoomian society with Lieutenant Turck's description of his own family history. The Turcks have been naval officers for generations—Jefferson's grandfather was an admiral—yet it is the custom of the family for each member to work his way up through the ranks, not to obtain commissions through education or influence.

Burroughs distinguishes human "types" by certain undefined hereditary qualities that are not simply those of race. Thus, while the Abyssinian army is led by a corps of highly intelligent and cultured officers, its common soldiery is composed of lesser men. This distinction is in accord with Burroughs's description of Africans in the Tarzan saga. Sometimes the Africans are portrayed as the most objectionable and cartoonish stereotypes. At other times they are depicted as intelligent, courageous, and highly civilized.

Burroughs was perceptive, and possibly ahead of his time, in recognizing that different peoples' ways of being civilized vary yet remain equally valid. There is a kind of "cultural relativism" implicit in *Beyond Thirty*, which is found in only a few of the better writers of Burroughs's day. More often one sees at least a tacit commitment to the "white man's burden," a moral imperative to spread Anglo-Saxon Christian principles throughout the world while riding roughshod over other cultures and traditions.

In contrast to this implicit racism and cultural imperialism, it is of note that Tarzan becomes an adopted member of the Waziri, a black African people. It is also of note that he becomes their chieftain—one hopes as a result of his intelligence, skills, courage, and naturally aristocratic nature and not merely because he is a white man among black men.

Burroughs was hardly consistent in his expressed attitudes but in commenting on this inconsistency we should remember that his writing career spanned a period of nearly forty years. His first stories appeared in the truly "lost world" that existed before the outbreak of the First World War. He continued to write throughout that war, the Jazz Age that followed, the Great Depression, the Second World War, and the earliest days of the Cold War. It is inevitable that he would change during that time, as did the world around him.

Burroughs's attitude toward war itself was inconsistent. In this regard it may be worthwhile to compare Burroughs with his contemporary and colleague, another immensely popular writer, Irvin S. Cobb (1876–1944). A native Kentuckian, Cobb worked initially as a journalist and then continued in that profession, sporadically, throughout his lifetime. He was also a radio personality and enjoyed a minor career as a character actor in films. Cobb's greatest success was as a short-story writer, and he was best known for a very long series of episodes concerning Old Judge Priest, which ran in the classic *Saturday Evening Post*. Judge Priest, an elderly, small-town magistrate by the time Cobb's stories take place, had been a soldier in the Confederate Army in the 1860s. Judge Priest and his cronies spend much of their time reliving their experiences in the Late Unpleasantness, their memories infused with a golden cloud of reminiscence and fantasy. Only in the story "Ex-Fightin' Billy" does Judge Priest personally denounce war.

Cobb himself was in Europe in 1914 when the First World War began. In an essay titled "Leaves Out of My Thrill-Book," he describes his experiences as a neutral journalist caught behind German lines. He expresses the terror of a flight in an observation balloon and his friendship with the German officer who invited him along and then his horror and grief when his new friend falls to a hideous death on his next flight.

In his short story "Field of Honor," Cobb describes the tragedy and degradation of the household of a Frenchman who is drafted into the army of his native land despite having emigrated to the United States. By telling the story of the horrors of war in this indirect manner, Cobb achieves a shattering effect.

Cobb's story "The Garb of Men," written while the war was still in progress, portrays a ruined world in which armies attack and retreat, march and counter-march, as civilization and all of its attributes slowly crumble into brute barbarism. One can almost imagine the utter ruin of Europe to which this seemingly endless war might have led: the world of *Beyond Thirty*. This is not to suggest that Burroughs read "The Garb of Men" and was inspired by it to write *Beyond Thirty*; such an idea is pure conjecture.

Oddly, while Cobb's attitude toward war manifests the shock of encountered reality in place of the golden-hazed fantasy of edited memory, Burroughs seemed to waver between a realistic portrayal of the carnage of war and the idealized jingoism and racism of *Tarzan and "The Foreign Legion"* (1947). The latter novel was written during the Second World War, when America fought simultaneously in Europe and Asia and when the official rationale for the desperate struggle was quite different, depending on whether one faced the Atlantic or Pacific Ocean.

In Europe the foe was Nazi Germany. The hate-filled racial propaganda and hideously genocidal policies of the Nazis provoked a reaction in which America portrayed itself as the champion of tolerance and universal brotherhood. In Asia the enemy was the Empire of Japan, and the foe was portrayed as a race of yellow-skinned, buck-toothed, treacherous subhumans. In *Tarzan and "The Foreign Legion"* Burroughs specifically refers to the Japanese as "monkey men."

The fact that thousands of loyal Japanese Americans fought and died for America further complicates the issue. In *Tarzan and "The Foreign Legion"* Burroughs simply picked up the nation's wartime propaganda message. Thus we can see that he did not progress linearly in his thought processes but took the proverbial two steps forward and one step back.

Still, in *Beyond Thirty* Burroughs can be seen stretching his creative talent as well as his political and social awareness. The description by Jefferson Turck of his own state of mind when appointed a personal slave of the Abyssinian commander is especially striking:

> Colonel Belik summoned me about seven o'clock to dress him for a function at the palace. In the midst of death and defeat the emperor was about to give a great banquet to his officers. I was to accompany my master and wait upon him—I, Jefferson

Turck, lieutenant in the Pan-American navy! In the privacy of the colonel's quarters I had become accustomed to my menial duties, lightened as they were by the natural kindliness of my master, but the thought of appearing in public as a common slave revolted every fine instinct within me. Yet there was nothing for it but to obey.

I cannot, even now, bring myself to a narration of the humiliation which I experienced that night as I stood behind my black master in silent servility, now pouring his wine, now cutting up his meats for him, now fanning him with a large, plumed fan of feathers.

As fond as I had grown of him, I could have thrust a knife into him, so keenly did I feel the affront that had been put upon me. But at last the long banquet was concluded. The tables were removed. The emperor ascended a dais at one end of the room and seated himself upon a throne, and the entertainment commenced. It was only what ancient history might have led me to expect— musicians, dancing girls, jugglers, and the like.

What more eloquent expression of Burroughs's most decent and empathetic impulse could there be? What more telling refutation of the apologias for slavery that were current in Burroughs's era and that, astonishingly and appallingly, still recur from time to time? "As fond as I had grown of him, I could have thrust a knife into him, so keenly did I feel the affront that had been put upon me."

Was Turck's enslavement an affront because he was white and his master black? Or did he refer to the affront that slavery itself places upon any enslaved person, regardless of color? In all likelihood it was a combination of the two, but one cannot be certain.

Burroughs himself was clearly of two minds with regard to the issue of slavery. In his foreword to *A Princess of Mars*, serialized in *All-Story* magazine four years prior to the publication of *Beyond Thirty*, Burroughs describes his great interplanetary adventurer, John Carter. He sets the stage by describing life at his own—that is, Burroughs's—home prior to the Civil War.

(John Carter) seemed always to be laughing and he entered into the sports of the children with the same hearty good fellowship he displayed toward those pastimes in which the men and women of his own age indulged; or he would sit for an hour at a time entertaining my old grandmother with stories of his strange, wild life in all parts of the world. We all loved him, and our slaves fairly worshipped the ground he trod.

Wait a minute!

Edgar Rice Burroughs seems to recall a childhood in the antebellum South. His family owned slaves, and John Carter was an "honorary uncle" of Burroughs? How can this be? Wasn't Burroughs born in 1875, the son of a minor industrialist? And wasn't he raised in Chicago? Why the Tara-like setting? And what's this about Burroughs's family's slaves worshipping the ground that John Carter walked on?

We might, I suppose, dismiss this fantasy as a narrative device, a frame such as many writers of Burroughs's generation used to set their stories. For that matter, the practice survives, although it is unusual in the present era. But that's too easy, I'm afraid. The Old South myth of gracious plantation life and happy, grateful, loyal slaves is purely that—myth. Whether Burroughs believed it or merely used it we cannot know nor, probably, does it matter. But we cannot help note that Burroughs placed himself—his fantasy self—in the aristocratic class. Few believers in natural aristocracy would define themselves as natural proles!

There is much to contemplate in *Beyond Thirty* and much to wonder about. Had Edgar Rice Burroughs read or seen a production of Shakespeare's great *Hamlet* when he wrote of the usurper murdering the king and marrying his widow in order to secure the throne for himself? Or is this parallel merely an amusing coincidence? And did Edgar Rice Burroughs ever encounter Irvin S. Cobb, perhaps during their mutual sojourn in Hollywood in the 1930s?

Did these two wealthy and lauded popular writers, each the son of a Civil War veteran, discuss their works together? Both wrote for *Argosy* magazine, although the bulk of Cobb's stories appeared in *The Saturday Evening Post* and other slick-paper magazines, while Burroughs remained a pulp writer from 1912 on into the 1940s. If they did meet, how one would love to have been a witness to their encounter. Cobb's father had served in the army of the Confederacy; Burroughs's in that of the Union. Did Burroughs know of Fightin' Billy Priest and did Cobb know of Capt. John Carter? Did these two authors share a moment of remorse over their early glorification of war and a thought of redemption in their rejection of that attitude?

It seems ironic that Cobb is almost forgotten today, except by scholars, literary antiquarians, and the residents of his onetime home of Paducah, Kentucky, where he remains a legend and a hero. Perhaps there will someday be a Cobb renaissance.

The Burroughs renaissance took place in the 1960s, and he has not been forgotten since. Copies of his major works—certainly the key Tarzan novels and the Martian series—reside on thousands if not millions of personal library shelves, and new printings continue to appear around the world. As for Burroughs's minor works, one of which in all candor *Beyond Thirty* must be considered, these too will reappear from time to time, providing modest pleasure for their readers as well as grist for the critical mill.